ASSASSINS

LAKE WORTH MYSTERIES

Written by Larry Alva

TABLE OF CONTENTS

CAST OF CHARACTERS

FLORIDA 1835

Aloyisus James, escaped slave and Seminole Indian

Steve Pierce, a barefoot mailman from Miami, Florida post office

FLORIDA PRESENT DAY

Ralph Graham, Attorney living in Lake Worth

Phyllis Graham, Ralph's wife, a Ukranian model

Jack Price, Private investigator, retired from the FBI

Anna Henderson, Private investigator, retired from the DEA

Detective Frank Guthrie, Palm Beach County Sheriff Detective

Sergeant Evans, PBC Sheriff Department, Lake Worth Substation

Ed Mobley, Lake Worth City Manager

Commissioner Ralph Nichols, Lake Worth City Commissioner

James Cameron, Developer

Commissioner Peters, Lake worth City Commissioner

Miles Thomas, waiter on Mr. Graham's yacht

James Hardesty, Mr. Graham's next door neighbor

David McKinley, Attorney and junior partner in Mr. Graham's firm

Michelle McKinley, David's wife

Mr. Bunting, Car accident victim

Palm Beach County (PBC) Sheriff

Phillip Summers, PBC Historian

Pastor James Morris, Pastor of a black church in south Lake Worth

Tom Morris, Pastor Morris' son

Michael Bellows, Attorney working for Mr. Cameron

Dmitri Filipov, bodyguard

Sergei Yureva, bodyguard

Victor Sidorov, Russian Oligarch

Director West, FBI Southeast Regional Director

PICTURES

Lake Avenue, Downtown Lake Worth

Dining on the Sidewalks, Lake Avenue

Lake Worth City Hall

Small sailboat in the Intracoastal
Waterway

Lake Worth Playhouse

PROLOGUE

1838 - Aloyisus James had been camped with other Seminole Indians, escaped slaves and criminals in the swamps and forests near the Loxahatchee River, west of present day Jupiter, Florida. Union troops had attacked the Seminole encampment and driven them back into the swamps, but the Seminoles moved through the swamps and returned fire with stolen rifles. They injured most of the Union officers, and caused the army to retreat back to Fort Jupiter. But Aloyisus knew they would be back. He took his Indian woman and headed south using a dugout canoe to paddle down the river. They traveled mostly at night and stayed away from the Union forces. When necessary they went overland through the forest and until they reached a large and meandering lake, fed by many streams. Aloyisus cut a tree, burned out a dugout canoe and paddled down the lake for many days. He landed on a palmetto covered island that bordered the muddy lake. The lake had fresh water that was muddy and brown from the many swamps. When he walked to the other side of the island, he saw a "Great Water" that he had only heard about. It stretched for as far as he could see. The wind raised waves that crashed against the island and made a sandy beach. There were small crabs and many birds. When he tried to get a drink, he spit out the water because it was salty. But he could see many small minnows in the surf, and he guessed that larger fish would be abundant. The muddy lake was present day Lake Worth, and the island was Palm Beach.

It seemed like he had been running forever, since he had escaped from the plantation in Georgia, and ran into the swamps. He had been helped by a loose band of renegade indians and runaway slaves, that were called Seminoles. They lived in the swamps of Southern Georgia, and Florida. James had been living with various bands of Seminoles for several years, and moving gradually south and east to find a better place to live. He was tired of running.

He and his woman built a lean-to from palm trees and cabbage palm leaves near the sandy shore. He fished and was pleased to find abundant fishing. He built a small fire and spent the night. The easterly breezes were pleasant, and he could hear the waves crashing on the other shore of the island. The days passed into weeks and then months. He increased the size of his lean-to, traded with other Indians that were traveling in canoes, and built a life on the island. Fishing was good on both sides of the island and they decided to stay.

Aloyisus worked to make his home more comfortable and more secure. He cleared a small patch of land on the island and planted a garden to provide vegetables. He learned it was better to plant in the fall and harvest in the spring, because of the extreme heat in the summer. He hunted for small game, on the island and on the far side of the Big Muddy. This provided more protein for his growing family. A child was born after two years, and three more followed. His woman died in child birth with the fifth child, and Aloyisus was forced to barter with a local tribe for a new woman to take care of his family. Life was hard, but it was better than being a slave or being an Indian in the swamps.

Many years later, a young barefoot white man walked up the beach and saw his fire. He stopped and introduced himself. "Hello, I am Steve Pierce, from the US Post Office in Miami". James was afraid and suspicious of white men, and he fingered the big knife in his belt. Pierce saw the motion and said, "you don't have to be afraid of me. I was sent to help settlers like you". "What can you do for me, James asked?" "I bring news of what is going on here in this land called Florida, and in the bigger United States. I have a one-page newspaper from Key West, that tells what is happening. I can also take and bring letters for you to people you may want to write". James said, "I can't write, and I don't want anyone to know where I am." Pierce said he understood, but offered to read him the news, if he could stay the night at his lean-to. James agreed, since Pierce had no weapons. Pierce became known as the "Barefoot Mailman" and he stayed with

James when he reached what would become Palm Beach Island.

On one trip, when the barefoot mailman walked by on the beach, he showed Aloyisus how to make a claim for the land and send it to the county seat in Key West. He said, "this way you will be able to claim this land for yourself and your family". The next morning, Pierce walked back south toward Miami with the land claim in his satchel. It would eventually get filed at the courthouse in Key West, and a copy was brought back to James by the postman. Aloyisus looked at the document with wide eyes when Pierce explained what it was. He could not believe that a slave could own anything, much less the land where he was now living. He kept the document in a safe place and passed it on to his son when he died.

CHAPTER 1:
FIRE

A party was going on a 100-foot yacht behind a large Lake Worth Beach mansion on the intracoastal waterway, across from Palm Beach Island. It was a beautiful starry night in South Florida. The temperature was comfortable, the moon was out, and a slight southeast breeze provided cooling for the guests on the rear and upper decks. The yacht was a 100 foot, Hatteras Avanti, with three main decks, 6 cabins, a huge main salon on the second deck and burnished teak throughout. Visitors entered from the rear of the yacht, up twin spiral staircases to the main deck. There was an open deck with an outdoor bar, and the main salon that you entered through sliding glass doors. The main salon was huge, with three large sitting areas, a two-story atrium, bar, dining room and 8-foot video screen. The salon was connected to the upper and lower decks by curved, ornate staircases. The upper deck had an open deck for lounging, pool, hot tub and captain's control center. A fly bridge above provided a second control center for the captain during docking maneuvers. The lower deck contained the cabins with in-suite baths, a game room, exercise rooms, and a spa. The crew quarters below the lower deck contained cabins for a crew of six, a full galley, the engine room containing two heavy caterpillar diesel engines and a wide variety of auxiliary equipment. The yacht also carried a 25-foot power boat to transport visitors. This yacht proclaimed a rich and powerful owner to all that saw her.

The mansion was a 10,000 square foot, two story, tile roof home, with Italian arches welcoming guests. The Italian style mansion took inspiration from 16th-century Renaissance architecture. It is also known as the Italianate style or Tuscan Villa style. The Italian villa, an impressive, square-towered, irregularly shaped mansion with deep eaves, was based on the northern Italian country houses of Tuscany. The style celebrated wealth and modernity, two characteristics widely embraced by a burgeoning upper and middle class.

The Italianate style first appeared in the US in the 1840s and became popular as an alternative to Greek Revival and Gothic design styles which were popular at the time. Italianate aesthetics were adapted to a range of building types and adapted for a range of income levels, including spacious homes on sprawling properties for the wealthy. Italian architecture is known for its use of warm tones. These hues create a very inviting and somewhat traditional style.

Guests walked through the large wooden double doors into the entrance hall that led to the great room and banquet room at the back of the house, looking out over the forever pool and dock on the intracoastal. The great room had tile floors with two large seating areas, leather furniture and expensive rugs. The banquet room had a large mahogany table, heavy wooden chairs that would seat twelve, and a sideboard that displayed antique English China. A large library was located to the left of the entrance and was used as an office/ reception room for business clients. The library had floor to ceiling oak bookshelves, a conference table and a spacious bar. The commercial style kitchen and a maid's quarters were located to the right.

The rooms had beautiful heavy Italian furnishings, and paintings styled after the old masters. A grand staircase led from the entrance hall to the upper floor, which contained six bedrooms with baths, a private sitting area and a music room.

You could hear the music and laughter from the rear patio of the mansion, as people drank and partied on the yacht. Midway through the party, the owner Ralph Graham asked everyone to assemble on the upper deck. Mr. Graham was wearing a white linen suit with a blue starched shirt and a gold tie. His alligator shoes, Rolex watch, and diamond ring were meant to impress. Mr. Graham said, "Thanks to all of you for coming tonight. I wanted to celebrate our latest legal victory with all of you. We took on the biggest firm in Miami and beat them. We could only do it because of the hard work, long nights and excellent legal research of many of the people here tonight. And my famous legal arguments helped too." The crowd laughed good naturedly at his obvious plug. "We have been building this firm, and our reputation is top notch. That means you can expect more fees coming our way, and more bonuses in your pocket. The sky is the limit people, and you can see that the sky looks bright tonight." There was applause and cheers from the crowd. "Now, let's all have a good time." The crowd spread out to all parts of the yacht, and the music restarted on the upper deck. Ralph and his wife, Melissa, circulated among the guests as the party continued.

Later, as the party started to wind down, people said their goodbyes and began leaving. Mr. Graham followed one of his best clients off the boat to show them the mansion and discuss future business. Two tall men dressed in black approached around the side of the mansion from the road. They were wearing black and had masks on their faces. They watched from the shadows as people began to leave and a beautiful woman went from the open deck into the main salon. Pulling silenced pistols, they moved up the rear stairs to the main deck. A waiter tried to stop them, and one of the men shot him without warning. The other man pulled a bottle from his coat, lit it and tossed the bottle into the main salon. The bottle broke with a crash and the main salon broke into flame from the molotov cocktail.

The spreading flames rushed over the ornate furnishings and upholstery in the main salon. The fire quickly spread inside the main salon so that the entrance doors could not be approached. Those caught in the salon rushed up the winding staircase to the upper deck before the fire reached them. The fire created black toxic smoke from the many flammable furnishings. As the people rushed up the stairs to safety, the smoke quickly spread throughout the salon and went down the staircase to the lower deck, trapping everyone in the cabins.

Quickly, the laughter from the crowd turned into screams. People began rushing off the boat and the two men joined with the crowd. They left the boat down the two back staircases as flames traveled throughout the boat. People called 911 and reported the fire as they watched the fire consume the big yacht. You could hear screams from the lower deck. The toxic smoke overcame any left on the yacht before the flames could reach them. Fire trucks came from downtown Lake Worth Fire Station with lights and sirens. The Fire Captain took control of the scene and asked if there were any people still on the yacht. Firemen tried to search the cabins, but the fire was too intense to reach them. The firemen connected the pumper to a nearby hydrant, laid out hoses from the street and sprayed water on both the yacht and the dock. This did not stop the flames, but it did prevent the fire from spreading.

The flames burned through the interiors and the decks, creating a massive cloud of smoke and flames. The heat buckled the steel plates of the yacht and threatened the large fuel tanks in the engine room. As everyone watched from a distance, you could hear small explosions from gasoline tanks and then a massive fire as several thousand gallons of diesel fuel burst from the tanks and burned. Finally, the flames died down as there was nothing left to burn. The smoking remains of the boat sank to the bottom of the shallow intracoastal waterway. The smoke and stench from the fire remained.

When the killers had safely gotten away from the scene, the first pulled an encrypted cell phone from his pocket and said, "It is done. We had to shoot a waiter, but we were not recognized or followed". "Make sure you are not followed and then come back here," a rough voice grated over the phone, and hung up.

CHAPTER 2:

LAKE WORTH BEACH

Jack Price was dressed in khaki slacks, a bright tropical shirt with dolphins and boat shoes on his size 12 bare feet. His long blond hair was pulled back into a ponytail, and he had a short well-trimmed mustache and goatee. Jack stood about 6 foot tall, with well-muscled arms and shoulders from many years in the military. He kept trim by running on the beach at least three days a week. Jack had worked with the FBI for over twenty years as a special agent after his military service. Assignments included federal criminal investigation, abductions, civil rights violations, and terrorist investigations after September 11th. He was retired and thoroughly done with the black suit, white shirt and tie uniform that screamed FBI agent. He still kept in contact with his FBI supervisor and had an FBI reserve badge, but these days he operated a private investigation business in Lake Worth Beach. He liked the variety of assignments that came his way, and the opportunity to relax between cases.

Jack was sitting across the table from his business partner, Anna Henderson, outside Murray's Irish Tavern on Lake Avenue in Lake Worth Beach, Florida. Anna was dressed in tight black slacks, with a white silk shirt open at the neck. She had carmel colored skin, long black hair and high-heeled shoes that made her taller than her normal 5 ft 8 in height. Anna's family was from the Caribbean, and she had joined the army out of high school. She was in the military police, where she learned all the fighting styles, and then joined the DEA as an undercover agent. Her assignments had included several years infiltrating and taking down drug cartel bosses in the US, the Caribbean, and Central America. After several difficult and dangerous assignments where she had been injured, she switched to DEA computer specialist before retiring from the agency. These days, she worked with Jack on special assignments, computer investigations and stake outs. She also maintained many contacts with the DEA and female military officers from her previous assignments.

Lake Worth Beach is a small eclectic town on the east coast of Florida south of West Palm Beach, with a population of about 35,000 residents, and a long history of strange and interesting residents. People from all walks of life come downtown to drink, eat at a wide range of restaurants and socialize. The town is known for its multicultural activities, including volunteer theater, fourth of July raft race, street art festival and pride-fest. Lake

Worth was known for rancorous politics, Hispanic immigrants, black communities and historical neighborhoods. It contains many small historical 2-bedroom bungalows, million-dollar mansions and everything in between. Whites, Blacks, Hispanics and multi-racial groups live in close proximity. This gives Lake Worth a vibrant and sketchy feel.

Lake Worth is separated into four sections geographically and economically. The Northeast quadrant contained multi-million dollar mansions near the water, and the College District where all the roads were named after ivy league universities. An eighteen-hole golf course was laid out on the water just north of Lucerne Avenue. The southeast quadrant contained upscale homes, multi-story condominiums and a large, abandoned hotel that people periodically tried to condemn or restore. It also contained two waterfront parks, with boat access. The northwest quadrant held a large park with baseball fields, many historical small bungalows, and several old churches. The southeast quadrant contained the traditionally black neighborhoods, a rundown park, old landfill, municipal utility facilities, and the Lake Worth High School. The main commercial district was located in the center of the city, from east to west along Lake and Lucerne Avenues. It held many restaurants, bars, shops and the historical theater. It also contained the City Hall, fire department, Sheriff substation and Arts District.

Jack and Anna were enjoying the results of the first day of the Lake Worth Street Painting Festival. Artists from throughout Southeast Florida were given an 8-foot square section of pavement on Lake or Lucerne Avenue. They used colored chalk to create fantastic works of art over a two day period, while thousands of festival goers admired their work. Today the weather had been good and many of the artists were nearing completion while lying on the warm pavement. This festival was a highlight of the year for Lake Worth residents, and a huge boost to the local tourism economy.

Murray's Irish tavern is located on a prominent downtown corner on Lake Avenue. They serve drinks and meals, both inside the restaurant and on the wide sidewalk in front. Live music was coming from the bar and the small dance floor. People and dogs sat outside at tables on the wide sidewalk. Jack and Anna were having drinks and dinner at an outside table while they watched people walk by on the sidewalk. Jack was doing his best to keep the relationship with Anna professional, but he definitely enjoyed being near her. Anna kept a tight rein on her emotions, but she noticed Jack's attraction with a smile. There were several tables with a large dog lounging under the table while its owners drank and enjoyed the music. Two thin men dressed in tight jeans and long-sleeved shirts strolled by arm in arm. Two motorcycle bikers sat at a table and drank beer while keeping an eye on their gleaming bikes parked at the curb. Everyone was happy and having a good time.

Suddenly, they heard sirens as fire trucks from the station four blocks away pulled out and went North on Federal Highway. Jack said, "I wonder what type of accident occurred on Federal Highway." They finished their meals, had a last drink, and then reluctantly separated. Jack said, "I will call you tomorrow if anything interesting comes up."

CHAPTER 3:
QUESTIONS

Detective Frank Guthrie from the Palm Beach County Sheriff's office responded to a dispatch call for shots fired and pulled up at a mansion located in northeastern Lake Worth Beach on the Intracoastal Waterway. Frank Guthrie was 45, 5'10" tall and heavily built, like the linebacker he was in high school, except with 30 extra pounds. He had steel gray hair and blue eyes that could bore through you. His suit was old and tired, and his shirt was wrinkled. He had come up through the Sheriff's office, starting at patrolman. He paid his dues on the streets, was promoted to sergeant, and then promoted to detective when he was 35. He had worked all over Palm Beach County, from western Boca Raton to Belle Glade. He was tough on his men but respected for his results. His cases included drug busts, fraud cases, and more recently, homicides. He was now the only detective at the Lake Worth Beach substation. He had watched younger men be assigned the more prestigious areas, such as Wellington or Palm Beach Gardens. He thought he was stuck in this small-town substation until his retirement came up in five years.

He still treated each case with the utmost professionalism and let the chips fall where they may. Perhaps, that was the reason he was not popular with the politicians that ran the county. As he got out of his unmarked white Ford Explorer Interceptor, he thought, "Here we go again".

Several other sheriff's cars and fire trucks were already there. He ducked under the crime scene tape being tied to trees and walked around the house toward the dock. A group of people were still milling around or standing in small groups in the backyard. The stink of burning oil and plastic was everywhere. Firemen were still hosing down flames on the yacht as it sat on the bottom of the intracoastal next to the dock. He asked a patrol sergeant what had happened. "They had a loud party, and a fire broke out on the boat. People panicked and ran off the boat. They were lucky it was at the dock. By the time the fire trucks responded, the boat was engulfed in flames".

"Did you get statements from the people at the party?" "I told the people at the scene to stay here until we took their statements. The people I talked to so far were drunk and I could not get good answers about how it happened. I did hear that shots were fired before the fire started". "Did you get a list of the people on the boat?" "Yes, I did, but some may have left before I came." "Were there any casualties?" "We won't know until we can search the boat. One person said he saw a man fall after the shots were fired. Several people heard screams when the boat was on fire." "Make sure you get statements from all of the people still here before you release them. If any saw anything important, hold them for me. Get patrolmen and divers out in the morning. We need to search the area and canvas the neighbors. Are the owners of the property still here?" "The husband is in the house. The wife was here during the party, but she is missing." "I will talk to the owner first. Bring any other witnesses to the house."

Detective Guthrie walked into the mansion from the back pool deck. He was impressed by the size of the home and the great room that was at the back of the house. He found one man sitting at the bar on one side of the large family room, staring out the window toward the smoldering yacht. He walked over, stuck out his hand and said," I am Detective Frank Guthrie from the Lake Worth Substation. I know this is a difficult time, but I need to ask you some questions." The owner turned and stared at him blankly, as Guthrie whipped out his identification. He said, "I am Ralph Graham, the owner of this place. This has been a terrible night, and I am not in the mood for questions." Guthrie responded, "I know this is difficult, but we need to ask a few questions now so we can help to find your wife. Can we sit down in a more comfortable spot?"

Graham nodded wearily and motioned him to a sitting area at the side of the bar with two heavy chairs and a small table. As they sat down, Guthrie began, "What happened tonight?" Mr. Graham said, "I am an attorney and partner of a firm in West Palm Beach. This week, we won a large case with a big fee, and I was having a party tonight to celebrate. I have a large yacht that I use for entertainment, and the party was held there. Everything was fine until after midnight. Some of the guests were leaving, and I walked back into the house with one of our major clients to discuss future business. While we were talking here in the great room, I heard people start to scream. I looked out the windows at the back of the house, and saw people running off the yacht, and flames on the boat. I ran outside and tried to get back on the boat, but the people were streaming down both rear stairways, and I needed to help them get safely to the dock. By that time, the whole main salon was a mass of flames. I yelled for someone to call 911. People were yelling and screaming as they ran. After most of the people were off the boat, I still heard a woman screaming. The yacht was a mass of flames by that time, and I couldn't even approach it. I didn't know who it was, but I will never forget those screams. The firemen finally came, and rigged hoses from the pumper at the street. By the time they started spraying water, the boat was engulfed in flames. They protected the dock, but the yacht burned and sunk in place as you can see."

Detective Guthrie asked, "when was the last time you saw your wife?" Graham replied, "She

15

was circulating through the guests on the yacht as I went into the house. She is a fantastic hostess, and she loved parties. She was wearing a black dress, and pearls that I had given her. After I saw the boat burning, I looked for her, but there was so much confusion that I don't know if she got off the boat safely. I am going crazy wondering if she was the woman screaming." Detective Guthrie asked, "Is there anywhere that your wife might have gone, since she did not come back to your house?" Graham said, "no, I don't know where she might be."

Guthrie asked, "Is there anyone that might want to hurt you or your wife?" Graham looked shocked as he said "no one would hurt my wife. She is a model, and everyone loved her. I am an attorney, and have many people that don't like me, but I can't imagine that any would attack me this way." "We will need a list of all your guests and employees that were here tonight, along with their contact information." "I will have my secretary send it to you tomorrow."

Detective Guthrie finished, "That is all we need for now. I will want to talk with you again. We will do everything we can to find your wife." The two men stood, shook hands and Detective Guthrie left the house. After checking with Sergeant Evans, he left instructions to follow up on the list of people at the party, preserve the crime scene, call out divers and CSI first thing in the morning, and canvas the neighbors. He then walked back to his Explorer and called his boss, the Palm Beach County chief of Detectives. He reported the basic facts of the fire and warned, this case will be front page news tomorrow. We are going to need extra resources. His boss growled, "A high profile attorney, can't we ever get a straightforward case?" Guthrie ended the call and started home. It would be a short night.

CHAPTER 4:

DETECTIVE GUTHRIE AND THE YACHT

The next morning, Detective Guthrie woke from a deep sleep as his alarm clock blared at 6:00 am. He rolled out of bed with a groan, showered and shaved, and dressed in another suit from his closet. Frank lived in Royal Palm Beach, which is a town in the western suburbs, with about the same population as Lake Worth Beach. His house was a four bedroom, single story home with a quarter acre lot in one of the many subdivisions. Frank was married with two kids, a boy in college, and his daughter in high school. He worried about the long hours away from his family, and knew they resented the time he spent at the office, but that was the job of a detective. His wife was setting out breakfast, making coffee and yelling at his daughter to hurry. He smiled as he tied his tie and walked into the kitchen. His wife asked, "Did you get a new case." He nodded, and grabbed a cup of coffee. "There was a big fire at one of the mansions and a yacht burned up. We are trying to find out if anyone was still on it." "Will you be home late again?" "I don't know yet, I will call you later." He munched on a bagel as he walked out the door and got into the Explorer. He liked being in the suburbs and knew that many policemen lived in Royal Palm Beach. But he didn't like the long commute to the Lake Worth Beach Sheriff substation.

Royal Palm Beach was on the western edge of the suburbs about fifteen miles west of West Palm Beach. It was a nice town, with good schools, plenty of shopping, churches and lots of restaurants. Deputies liked to live in the suburbs, since they saw the problems that occurred in the city. Frank and his wife had lived there for twenty years, and he hoped to retire there. As Frank drove south on Crestwood and turned east on Southern Boulevard, a main east-west corridor, he thought about how his baby daughter was becoming a young woman. He shuddered a little and promised himself he would take more time with her before she went off to college. He would check out any boy that tried to date his little girl, and the Sheriff car in the driveway should make them think twice.

As Frank was driving into the office, he called Sergeant Evans. Evans told him the Sheriff divers were scheduled to be at the mansion that morning to search the burned yacht. He told Evans to meet the divers and have them first look for bodies, and then for fragments from the firebomb. He would continue interviewing witnesses at the substation.

The PBC Sheriff Substation was a white two-story building located north of Lucerne Blvd and just east of the FEC railroad tracks. There was a small parking lot for the public and a larger lot in back for deputies. The public entrance was through a single door on the side of the building that led to a receptionist behind a glass window. After providing identification and a reason for the visit, visitors were allowed into a small reception area with pictures of the Sheriff, flags and wanted posters. Sheriff personnel would either talk to the visitors by phone or ask them to come upstairs for a meeting. A slow elevator took them upstairs, where there were rows of gray government desks that looked twenty years old, a few small conference rooms and coffee machines. The detectives offices were located at the back of the building along with the Sheriff Captain in charge of the substation.

About noon, Evans called Guthrie. "Boss, the divers searched the remains of the boat, and found two bodies. They are bringing them out now." "OK, I will be there in fifteen minutes. Is the coroner there now?" "Yes, I will hold the bodies here and put up a tent to provide some privacy." Frank walked downstairs to the parking lot, jumped in the Explorer, and drove north to the Graham mansion. When he walked behind the mansion, he saw the tent and a cluster of people within the taped off crime scene. He said hello to the coroner and asked him what he had learned. "The two bodies are a male and a female. Both were badly burned as a

20

CHAPTER 5:

COMMISSIONER NICHOLS

Ed Mobley, the City Manager for Lake Worth Beach was sitting at Henry's on the Beach restaurant for breakfast. Henry's was located on the Lake Worth Beach pier and had two floors for dining, as well as pier side tables and a bar on the beach. The second floor had a screened in dining area with views in three directions of the beach and ocean. This morning there were only a few guests upstairs, which would make it easier for Ed to meet with Commissioner Nichols. It was a beautiful morning with the beach, the sand and the surf. The breeze from the southeast was enough to raise a 2-foot surf, which lapped gently on the beach. There were already many families on the beach, with their chairs, umbrellas and kids. And Ed kept his eye out for the pretty girls parading along the waterline in various colors of bikinis.

Ed was 40, 6' 1" tall, with brown hair and brown eyes. He had some Italian ancestory and fancied himself a modern-day pirate. He had sailed a 44-foot Morgan sailboat through the Caribbean as a young adult, and then had settled down to work in several small-town city governments. He was good at bringing a wide variety of people together and was fair to all political views. He was looking forward to a long career in Lake Worth Beach, but he knew that would only happen if he could keep in the good graces of at least three of the four elected commissioners and the mayor.

Commissioner Nichols finally arrived and sat down at the table. He was 35, 5'8" tall, with balding hair and a noticeable beer belly. He loved to talk with anyone and had been a commissioner for seven years. He acted like he was always running for election, and that had made him successful in the political wars in Lake Worth. He was also careful to keep on the good side of the city business community that provided the lion's share of donations for his campaign.

The waitress came and served both coffees. She gave them menus and disappeared to get the drinks." How is it going Ralph?" "Things could be better. We got a real surprise with the election in November. I thought for sure we would be able to keep our three-person majority, but that new guy, Peters, looks like he could be trouble." "Well, Ralph, I have to work with all the commissioners. I will be as fair with you as I am with him." "You may want to reconsider that position. If the tree huggers get three votes, you won't last long. We have many planned projects in the city and many of them won't be approved unless we keep the three-man majority. We have run the city for the last 7 years and have made good things happen. That could change quickly and destroy everything we have planned." "Peters used the environmental card to win the election, but he seems reasonable and willing to listen to all sides. You may not get everything you want, but we should be able to work out suitable compromises." I don't want compromises, we need to win these votes, so we can keep the party going."

Their meals came and they were both quiet. But the mood was now somber. The beautiful beach did not change that.

CHAPTER 6:

RALPH GRAHAM

Jack Price woke groggily. He slowly rolled out of bed. He stepped into the living room of his two-bedroom bungalow. Bottles, cans and boxes of old food were sitting everywhere. It smelled like last night's fish dinner and beer. He picked up his ringing cell phone from the table and answered, "Price Investigations." A man's voice said, "Are you ok? Your voice sounds slurred. It's 10 o'clock. Is this your office?" "Jack answered, what can I do for you?" "My name is Ralph Graham. I live in Lake Worth Beach on the Intracoastal. There was a fire on my boat last night. My wife is missing and could have been on the boat during the fire. I heard that you could find out what really happened." "I will be right out to your property. Can I meet you there at about noon?" "Yes, I will be here." Graham gave price the address and then disconnected.

Jack's bungalow was one of many historical houses in the northeast quadrant of Lake Worth. It was painted green with white trim and was built in the 1920's. It sat on a narrow lot on D Street, with a front porch, living room, kitchen, bath and two bedrooms inline. The back rooms were connected by a narrow hall with a back door leading into a small backyard with palm trees and a fire pit. Jack had lived there for ten years and was very comfortable as a bachelor.

Jack showered, put on Chino pants, a blue dress shirt and his boat shoes. He went outside, hopped in his black BMW, and headed to Good Time Restaurant on Lake Avenue near Federal Highway for coffee and breakfast. After breakfast, he headed north on Federal Highway, east on Duke Drive at the far northeast corner of Lake Worth and turned north on Holy Cross Lane. He stopped at the address Mr. Graham had given and looked at the size and style of the mansion. The mansion was a two story, Italian style home that stretched over most of the property frontage. The arches across the front of the house and the large double wooden front doors showed this was not an ordinary home. He smiled to himself. Clearly, these people had money.

He could smell the fire from the road. He walked to the door, rang the bell and introduced himself when Mr. Graham came to the door. Graham had shorts and a rumpled shirt which looked like he had slept in them. Graham would normally have been an imposing figure. He was 6'2" tall, about fifty, with broad shoulders, a fit body and silver hair. Jack could imagine him in a courtroom. His voice was strong, even though Jack could tell he had been drinking.

Jack said, "what happened here?" Graham replied, "let's go back to the boat". They walked through the big house and out the back door past the pool. The yacht was sunk at the dock. It still smoked and gave off a foul smell.

Graham said, "we were having a party to celebrate a case that I won. All my staff and the neighbors were invited. We were having a good time and the party was winding down. I went into the house to say goodbye to some of my staff that were leaving. Phyllis, my wife, stayed on the boat with our other friends. Suddenly, I heard screams coming from the back yard. A fire broke out on the boat. By the time I got back out to the boat, people were screaming and running. I got to the main deck but could not get into the main salon on that deck due to the fire. We could hear screams like a woman. I don't know if it was Phyllis or someone else. I need you to find out what happened and why." He started to break down but held his emotions in check.

Jack started with his preliminary questions. "Do you have any enemies?" "I am a lawyer and have many cases. Take your pick. I don't think they would try to kill me." "We will do everything we can to solve this case. I will keep you informed. I also will need to talk with you in more detail soon.".

Jack could tell Mr. Graham was still in shock and decided to wait for more detailed questions in a more controlled environment. He said, "I will get back with you and make an appointment where you can give your statement about the fire. If you think of anything important before then, please call me". He left his card, said goodbye and walked around the house to the road.

As Price left the house and headed to the office he thought this could be the big one. His cases had been small lately, and this one could be the kind of case that could make his reputation and his bank account.

CHAPTER 7:

DEVELOPER AND COMMISSIONER MEETING

James Cameron was a tall, good-looking man with a $2000 handmade suit and silk tie. He was a high-end developer of real estate projects throughout southeast Florida. He walked into the famous West Palm Beach restaurant and said to the Maitre'd, "Hello Charlie, I see you are having a good lunch crowd. Is my table ready? I'm expecting a guest." The Maitre'd quickly led him to a secluded table near the windows with a view on Okeechobee Boulevard. He seated him, waved over a waiter in a starched uniform with a towel over his arm. "Would you like your normal drink sir?" "Yes, on the rocks, make it a double." The drink came quickly, and he sat back in his plush chair to look at the menu.

The restaurant was the best in town and part of a nationwide chain. It was fashioned after a British men's club, with heavy wood and red velvet furnishings. A fancy bar, with heavy chairs and small tables was meant for guests to meet for drinks. After the bar, the hallway led back to a large dining room, with larger tables covered in linen, large dining chairs, and beautiful artwork. The dining room looked out over Okeechobee Boulevard, which was the main entrance to West Palm Beach. It was across the street from the City Convention Center, so that it attracted many visitors. The kitchen was through double swinging doors, so that the waiters could efficiently serve their guests. The kitchen was large with stainless steel furnishings, and plenty of room for several chefs to prepare their specialties. Three-inch-thick steaks, lobsters, king crab legs and fresh fish were always on the menu. Fresh beef and seafood were flown in every day, and there were no prices on the menu. Only the best liquors and wines were served.

In a few minutes, the Maitre'd came over leading a heavy-set man with balding hair, wearing an off-the-rack suit with no tie. Cameron wrinkled his nose, but quickly recovered his smooth smile. He greeted the man, "glad you could make it Nichols. Thanks for taking the time." "I always take the time to meet my constituents, especially when the scotch is good, and the steaks are thick." They sat and Nichols ordered a double scotch. They looked over the menus and selected filet mignon medium rare. When the waiter left, they talked for a few minutes and then Cameron got down to business.

"Ralph, the pool and casino complex on Lake Worth Beach has been losing money for years. People clamor about the pool being reopened, but nobody uses it. The casino building next door has been underused from the start." "That complex is a pain in the ass," said Nichols, "but the old-timers are dead set on keeping it. They make up a lot of campaign donations."

"Well, I can guarantee your campaign donations if you help me buy and redevelop that property. It will bring money into the town from tourism on the beach. I can build a high-rise hotel on the beach where the pool is located. The casino building will be used for parties and meetings of people staying at the hotel." "There will be a lot of opposition," said Nichols. "It won't matter if we have three votes. Can you deliver or not?" "Three votes were solid last year, but the damn tree hugger won District 2 in November and I don't know what the district 4 commissioner will do." "Well s***, you better find out and put together an airtight majority. There are millions to be made if you play it right."

The steaks came and they were huge. They each ordered another drink and started eating. The rest of the meal they talked about politics and the stock market. As Cameron said good-bye and left the restaurant, he did not like the sound of Nichols' statements. I wonder if there is another way? I am not going to let this deal sour because of a few tree-huggers. Let me see what I can do.

When Cameron got back to his office, he closed the door and made a phone call. A guttural voice snarled, "What do you want?" Cameron said, "You know that project we were going to use to launder your money? I am having trouble getting it off the ground." "What seems to be the trouble? I thought it was all set." "There was an election, and Commissioner Peters was elected. He is a tree-hugger and doesn't want to play ball with the old majority. Can you convince him?" A short silence followed. Then the voice said, "Done."

CHAPTER 8:

FIRST DETECTIVE MEETING

Jack Price picked up Anna from the Boynton Pass marina on South Federal. The marina was directly west of the Boynton Inlet, which provided access to the Atlantic Ocean from the south end of Lake Worth. The marina had dock space for large boats and yachts on four finger docks. There were facilities and a rolling crane to lift out yachts up to fifty feet length, and store them in a paved lot. A 200 foot by 300 ft warehouse, 24 feet high, held hundreds of power boats that could be placed in the water by huge fork lift trucks. There were boat cleaning and maintenance services, as well as showers and toilets for liveaboards. A ship store provided boating needs and fuel. There was even a tiki hut and picnic tables for evening parties. It was a convenient location for Anna to keep her sailboat docked, so that she could access the intracoastal waterway or the Atlantic Ocean.

Jack drove his BMW to the Palm Beach County Sheriff Office (PBSO) substation located on Lucerne Ave in Lake Worth Beach, just east of the

Florida East Coast (FEC) railroad tracks. The FEC tracks handled heavy freight trains as well as the new high-speed Brightline trains. The rumbling of trains could be felt inside the substation.

The PBSO substation is an old white two story commercial office building. Jack pulled into the small parking lot next to the railroad tracks, and they walked to the entrance. There was a small reception area inside the front door, with a locked door to enter the rest of the building. There were pictures of past and present sheriffs, public safety posters and a receptionist station located behind bullet proof glass. Jack walked to the receptionist window and told her he had an appointment with Detective Guthrie. The receptionist called upstairs while Jack waited, and spoke for a few minutes. She then turned back to Jack and Anna. "You may go up now. The elevator is at the end of the hall. Go to the second floor and Detective Guthrie will meet you there."

Jack and Anna were buzzed through the locked door and then waited as the old elevator doors screeched open. They walked into the elevator and hit the button for the second floor. An old hydraulic pump wheezed as it slowly raised the elevator to the second floor. When the doors opened, they were greeted by Detective Guthrie shaking their hands. He led them back through the long shabby hall to his conference room. The conference room had an old metal conference table with scars from many long meetings. There were eight straight back metal desks, a metal file cabinet with a coffee machine on top, and a large white board on the back wall. Lots of file folders, papers and pictures were on the table.

"Would you like coffee", he asked? "No thanks, we just finished some. I know what kind of coffee you have in police stations". "Well, you could have brought me a cup", said Guthrie. Jack, Anna and Detective Guthrie sat at the table. Sergeant Evans came into the room with an envelope that had a stack of photos in it. He kept standing, and started to tape the photos on the white board. Detective Guthrie said, "Ok, let's see what we have to start the investigation. Normally, Jack, you would not be allowed here, but Mr. Graham specifically asked that you be included in the investigation. Hopefully, we can make better progress if we both work together. We will be recording all meetings on the case."

"The first victim was a male waiter on the yacht, by the name of Miles Thomas. He was about 30 years old and worked on the yacht as a mate and waiter. He was evidently in the wrong place at the wrong time on the rear deck of the yacht. Witnesses have said that they saw two tall men, dressed in black come up the aft stairway from the dock about midnight. They both had gloves and masks to prevent them being recognized. One shot the waiter as he started to question them. The second threw a molotov cocktail through the open doors on the main deck, into the main salon. The bottle broke on the marble floor in the main salon and started the fire. The two men then turned and ran off the yacht as the other passengers panicked. No one saw where they went."

"The second victim was a woman about 30, well dressed in a black dress. She was found by divers in the aft cabin, after the boat sank and the fire was out. We don't have an identity yet, and will wait for the coroner's report for a cause of death."

"Then, we have Mrs. Phyllis Graham. She is the wife of the property owner, Mr. Ralph Graham. We obtained a picture of her from her husband. She was on the yacht at the time of the fire, and is currently missing. Mr. Graham is very concerned that she may be the woman found in the aft cabin."

"Several of the guests have been identified and interviewed. Many were drunk at the time, and we have different accounts of what happened. The burned yacht is lying on the bottom beside the dock, under about three feet of water."

"Mr. Graham was in shock when we talked to him, and didn't help much. We will have to talk with him again. We need to find Mrs. Graham or identify her as the woman that died."

Jack said, "Graham mentioned several cases where he may have made enemies. We need to get his office to provide a list of clients, and the case files." Guthrie continued, "we also need to get more background on both Mr. and Mrs. Graham. We need to know what she did before and after she was married. What was her relationship with Mr. Graham? It wouldn't be the first time that a husband killed his wife. We need to know if there was life insurance, and what was their financial situation."

Anna said, "Were there any enemies from the neighborhood, or could this be a robbery gone wrong? These mansions are only a few blocks from some rough areas. We need to check if there have been recent break-ins nearby."

They made assignments for different teams to take different parts of the case. Detective Guthrie took Frank Graham, his clients and the people at the party. Jack took Mrs. Graham and her modeling contacts in New York. Afterward, Jack sat back and said, "this case has way too many suspects. We need to narrow them down, before we can make progress". Guthrie replied, "hopefully, we can verify some of the alibis and shorten the list." Guthrie said," let's meet again in two days and see where we are." They all got up and trooped out of the conference room.

CHAPTER 9:
MR. GRAHAM'S
CLIENTS AND FRIENDS

Sergeant Evans spent the next day contacting the list of friends and clients that had been at the Graham party. He made appointments for interviews at the substation starting in the afternoon and going into the next day. It was important to get statements from each potential witness as soon as possible so that their stories could be compared and checked. Both Guthrie and Evans conducted the initial interviews. Evans took the friends from the community and Guthrie took the business associates and clients. Sergeant Evans started with the next-door neighbor.

"Good afternoon. Please state your whole name for the record." "James Hardesty" "Where do you live currently?" "Just north of the Graham mansion on the corner of the C-51 canal and the intracoastal." "How long have you lived there?" "We moved in five years ago." "Tell me what you saw at the Graham party." "We walked over to the party about 10:00 pm after coming back from dinner, saw Phyllis greeting guests as they arrived, and circulated as we said hello to neighbors. About 11:00 pm, Ralph gave a short speech about winning a big lawsuit. About midnight, several guests were leaving when we saw two men in dark clothing come up the rear stairs to the main deck from the dock. A waiter started toward them, and they shot him. My wife screamed and we ducked behind some tables that we overturned. One man covered the crowd with his pistol while the other reached in his coat, pulled out a bottle that looked like wine, lit the rag hanging out of it and threw it into the main salon. The bottle broke, and flames spread quickly from the bottle to the draperies and carpeting of the salon. The men turned and went down the rear stairs to the dock. As soon as I thought it was safe, we ran to the stairs, and got off the boat too. By that time, the whole inside of the yacht was in flames. We were able to get away and we called 911 to report the fire. We stood around for a while, but there was nothing we could do to help, so we went home." "Did you recognize the two men?" "No, they were both tall, white and had masks." "Do you know of anyone in the neighborhood that dislikes the Grahams?" "No, they are excellent neighbors, and we have a lot of fun together." "Thank you for your time, if you think of anything else, please call me at the number on my card."

Detective Guthrie interviewed Mr. Graham's clients and business associates. "Good afternoon, we are conducting interviews of everyone at the Graham party. We appreciate your cooperation.

The interviews are normal procedure when people have been at a crime scene, so that we can gather information and exclude them from further investigation. For the record, what is your name?" "I am David McKinley." "How do you know Mr. Graham?" "I am a junior partner at his firm and help him with some of his legal cases." "Please tell me what happened when you went to the Graham party." "My wife and I went to the party about 9:30 pm. The legal case we had been fighting was exhausting, and it was nice to be able to relax at the party together. We were welcomed by the Grahams and then mingled with other guests. I knew several of them from the office. We had drinks and snacks on their beautiful yacht. You could tell he was the senior partner and took home the lion's share of the fees. There were a lot of people, and we went to the upper deck to enjoy the stars and the view of the intracoastal. About 11:30 pm, Melissa said she was tired and was going below for a few minutes. I knew she had several drinks, and thought she needed to freshen up. I got involved in a conversation about football and forgot the time. About midnight, I heard something that sounded like a shot, and then I heard glass breaking. We didn't know what had happened but heard screaming on the main deck. People were yelling fire, and we all wanted to get off the boat. I tried to go down the main salon steps, but the fire in the salon was too hot. Luckily, there were rear stairs to the main deck and from there we took the rear spiral stairs to the dock. I thought that

Melissa had probably been on the main deck and had left the boat before me. I searched for her all over the back yard but didn't find her. She may have gone home with one of her girlfriends if she was not feeling well. I didn't really see much after I left the yacht, except for the firemen. I knew the yacht was a total loss. I looked for Melissa for another hour, and then went home to see if she was there. I haven't seen her since the party. Can you help to find her." "Mr. McKinley, we will do everything we can to find your wife. What was she wearing, and do you have a picture I could borrow?" "She was wearing a black party dress and high heels. Here is a picture. Please give it back when you are done." "Thank you for your help and we will be in touch soon. Here is my card." Frank thought to himself, now we have two missing women.

At the end of the day, Sergeant Evans and Detective Guthrie had completed interviews for most of the people on board the yacht during the party. The rest would wait for another day. They left the substation and had a drink at Dave's Sports Bar on the corner of Jog Road and Forest Hill. It was outside their jurisdiction, so they could relax. Frank wanted a second drink, but knew the family was waiting. He said goodbye and headed home.

CHAPTER 10:
MRS. GRAHAM DISCOVERED

Anna Henderson, Jack's friend and partner in his private investigation business, was sitting in the dark in the cockpit of her 35 ft Catalina sailboat anchored 200 yards from the burned yacht. She used the sailboat as a home and also used it for surveillance when necessary. No one took notice of a sailboat anchored in the intracoastal waterway.

The sailboat had a furling mainsail and furling jib, so the boat could be operated by one competent sailor. The boat had a cockpit that could easily hold six people, cockpit table, compass, GPS display and radios. The main cabin was down a ship's stairs. It held a U-shaped seat and table, bench seat, galley stove, sink and refrigerator, running water and chart table. There was a forward berth for two people, a forward bathroom and shower. The captain's quarters were in the rear under the cockpit. They contained a queen-size bed, bath and shower. Overall, the boat was a good cruiser for long distances, and a comfortable home in port. Anna had been as far as Key West and back.

Tonight, she wore black tactical slacks, a black hoodie and black deck shoes. She kept the lights off and watched the Graham mansion and the boat dock through a night vision scope while she slipped a beer from the fridge. Jack had asked her to watch the Graham mansion. Perhaps the killer would come back to the scene of the crime. It was a warm evening and clouds were threatening rain. The seabreeze fell off and only gentle waves rocked the boat. The lights were off at the Graham mansion and everything on the waterfront was quiet. It was going to be a long night.

Suddenly, she spotted motion on a boat three houses down from the Graham mansion. The boat was a 40-foot Carver Cruiser that was completely dark. A figure emerged from the salon and peeked out on the dock. It was hard to see details. Someone was there. Was the owner getting high, was he bedding his girlfriend, or was this something else more sinister?

Anna raised her camera outfitted with night vision and took several quick shots. She waited as the dark figure reappeared. The figure stepped to the dock, looked around and slowly moved to shore. Then he slowly slipped from one shadow to the next toward the Graham dock. Anna took more pictures and could not get a clear picture of the face. What was he going to do, set another fire or try to kill Mr. Graham? Anna had no way to quickly investigate from the anchored sailboat.

Anna called Price. Jack was walking down Lake Avenue from a late-night dinner and drinks when he heard his cell phone ring. "What's up?" "Someone is at the Graham house. They came off a boat three houses down and now they are checking the boat fire. I can't tell who it is. Will you check it out?" Jack said, "I will be there in five, hold tight and take more pictures."

Jack turned and ran back to the parking lot on H street. He jumped into his black BMW and headed up Federal, ignoring the lights on the way. Nothing was happening as he took a sharp right on Duke and parked a block from the Graham house. As he walked fast, he checked the Walther 9mm pistol on his hip and let his eyes adjust to the dark. He called Anna, "Where is the guy now?" "He went back to the neighbor's boat, and I don't see him now." Jack said, "I will check it out. Let me know if you see anything."

Jack walked quietly through the Graham yard. All the houses along the water Were dark. He worked his way along to the cruiser parked three doors down. He stopped at the dock and watched in silence. "Is anything moving?" he asked Anna on the phone. "No, but someone is still there on the cruiser." He approached cautiously. Stepping on someone's boat was like walking into a house and he did not want to find an angry owner with a gun. But he could not let a killer get away. Finally, he saw the outline of a figure on the rear deck of the cruiser, looking out over the water. He pulled his pistol, stood behind a dock post and said, freeze, put your hands up. The figure jumped and turned quickly, but then gradually put his hands up. "Don't shoot, I am not armed", said a voice cowering with fear. The voice was of a woman instead of a man, and she started crying. Jack quickly moved to the boat, pulled her hands behind her and bound them with flex ties.

The figure was clearly a woman dressed in black sweatpants and a black sweatshirt. She was about 5 ft 8 in tall, but he could not tell her features in the dark. "Who are you?" "My name is Phyllis Graham. I was almost killed two nights ago". "Then why are you here?" "I managed to crawl out the forward hatch and slip over the side of the boat after it caught fire. I could hardly breathe. I was afraid the killers were still there and would try to kill me, so I swam to this boat." "I am not going to hurt you", Jack said. He quickly searched her for weapons and ID. After he confirmed she had no weapons and identified her from a picture Mr. Graham had given him, he cut the flex ties. She rubbed her wrists. "Who are you?" "I am Jack Price, a private investigator your husband hired". He held out his credentials so she could see. "Now start from the beginning. What happened that night"?

"We were having a party on the boat to celebrate a big case. We invited neighbors and my husband's partners to come over for drinks. There were lots of people coming and going. By midnight, people were leaving, and I stepped through the main salon and went down the stairs to the bow head. Suddenly, I heard a bottle break in the main salon and smelled smoke. When I opened the door of the head, I saw smoke and flames all over the stairs to the main salon. I screamed for help, but no one came. I could not go back that way, so I went forward. I was able to crawl onto the bed and reach the latch for the front hatch. The heat and smoke were terrible by that time. I barely slipped out through the hatch onto the front deck. The boat was engulfed in flames. I was afraid that the people who burned the boat were still there. I slipped over the side and swam to this boat. I knew the owners were gone and I crawled up on deck. I hid here catching my breath and watching the flames".

"Why didn't you go to the house and call the police?" "I did not know who wanted to kill us, and whether Ralph was alive or dead. I just stayed here. No one would find me. I must have fallen asleep and woke up the next morning cold and wet. I was able to find these clothes and some food in the boat. Tonight, I finally decided to go back to the burned boat and thought you had come back to kill me. How is Ralph?" "He is okay but is worried about you". "I did not know what to do but was afraid to go back to the house. Killers could be watching." "I think you were smart. You should not take more chances. Is there a place you have that is safe?" "No, I can't go to a hotel because someone will

47

recognize me." "Okay, you can stay with my friend for a few nights. She will keep you safe."

Jack called Anna, gave her an update, and asked her to head back to her marina. Turning back to Mrs. Graham, he said, "My female partner has a nice sailboat with two berths in a local marina. You will be safe there until we figure this out. I'll take you there now and we can get something to eat on the way." Mrs. Graham nodded and said, "I am starving." Jack led her to his BMW.

They drove to a Denny's restaurant in West Palm Beach that stayed open all night. After they both had large portions of bacon, eggs and pancakes, While Mrs. Graham was in the restroom, Jack called Mr. Graham to let him know that his wife had been found and left a message on Detective Guthrie's phone. He then drove Mrs. Graham to the marina to meet Anna. Anna quickly reassured Mrs. Graham and made her comfortable on the sailboat. "We will sort out this further tomorrow morning after everyone has had some rest." Mrs. Graham gladly took a shower, borrowed some clothes and went to sleep.

CHAPTER 11:

ANNA'S BOAT

The next morning, Jack drove his BMW to the Graham mansion, to tell Mr. Graham that he had found Mrs. Graham safe. Jack still thought of Graham as a key suspect, and that is why he did not take Mrs. Graham back to her house immediately.

Jack walked to the front door, rang the bell and waited for the maid to let him in. She said Mr. Graham was by the pool. The pool was rectangular, with blue tile above the water line and light blue "Everbrite coating below. It measured about 16 feet by 24 feet, with a light brown tile deck around the pool. An outside bar and grill was in one corner of the tile deck.

Mr. Graham looked like he had had a rough night and was already nursing a drink by the pool. When he saw Jack, he got to his feet and asked, have you found anything new? Jack and Graham sat down, and Graham asked the maid to bring them both coffees. After they were served, the maid left, and Jack explained that they had found Mrs. Graham hiding on a neighbor's boat three doors south from the mansion. "Why on earth would she go there and not go back to the house?" "She was afraid that the killers were still in the area, and that you might have been killed also."

Mr. Graham was overjoyed that his wife was alive but confused why she had not come back sooner. "I don't understand who or why someone would attack us like this," he said. Jack replied, "this may be a good strategy for a while. If someone is trying to kill you or your wife, it may be safer to have them think she is dead. Do you have anywhere you could go with her that you both would be safe." "Yes, I will make arrangements myself and not tell anyone else". "OK, I will talk to Mrs. Graham and bring her back here".

Jack walked back through the house, said goodbye to the maid, and jumped back in the BMW. He drove south on Federal past downtown Lake Worth to the marina. It was a busy day at the marina, with boats being moved into and out of the water from inside or outside storage locations. The marina had the capacity to lift boats up to 60 feet long for storage or repair. They also had a ship's store, restrooms and docks for boats on the water.

Jack walked down to Dock B and made his way to the Catalina sailboat. He could see Anna in the cockpit and waved at her. "Permission to come aboard, Captain?" he said. She smiled and waved a cleaning rag at him. Jack couldn't keep his eyes off

Anna. She looked good, even in shorts and a tee shirt. He quietly climbed on the boat, and asked, "how is she doing?" "Everything was quiet. I took her breakfast a half hour ago." "Good, we need to get some answers". Anna walked down the cabin steps and through the main cabin to the front berth. She gently knocked on the door and asked, "Mrs. Graham, how are you feeling this morning?" "I am better now than I was on that other damn boat. Thanks for the breakfast and coffee". "Jack is here to see you". Mrs. Graham said she would be up in a few minutes. Anna said, "I left some clothes for you if you would like to change. I think we are similar in size." Mrs. Graham thanked her and said she would be right up. Anna went back to the cockpit to talk with Jack.

After about fifteen minutes, Mrs. Graham climbed up the ship's stairs from the cabin and walked to the cockpit. She was wearing a brown pair of shorts, blue blouse and sandals. Her hair was combed and pulled back in a ponytail. Jack noticed that she was stunning, even without make-up. Mrs. Graham took a seat in the cockpit across from Jack and Anna. Jack started, "Mrs. Graham, I need to ask you some questions to get to the bottom of this murder case". "Murder, I'm Not Dead. What else happened on the boat?" "A man was shot on the deck of your yacht and a woman about your age and build was found in the aft cabin. She was trapped by the fire and died from the smoke. Divers found her when they searched what was left of the boat.

The sheriff thought it was you when they recovered the burned body. Your husband said you were missing." "Do you know who was in that aft cabin?" "Oh no! I saw Melissa go downstairs before I did. She had been drinking and said she didn't feel well. If she died because of us, I would feel terrible". "What was Melissa's last name?" "It was Melissa McKinley. She is or was the wife of a lawyer working with Ralph on his cases." "Do you know of anyone who would want to hurt you?" "No, most of my friends live in New York and no one here would hurt me. There are people in Lake Worth Beach that steal from the large mansions, but we have never had trouble like that."

"Does Mr. Graham have any enemies?" "Well, he is a powerful attorney that has won many cases. The cases hurt many people. Some of them might want to get even. I don't know much about his legal business. You would have to ask him. Do you think someone is trying to kill us?" Jack replied, "Well, guns and Molotov cocktails are no joke. Whoever did it, killed a man and a woman. The sheriff will want to talk with you and your husband about that".

"I am so scared. Can't we keep this a secret for now?" "I have talked with your husband, and we agree it would be good for you two to lay low until this case is solved. I will take you to him now and he is making arrangements for someplace safe. We will need to talk to both of you again once you get settled."

Jack waited until Mrs. Graham had collected her few belongings and said Goodbye to Anna. Then he drove her back to the Graham mansion. Ralph was already packing clothes and supplied in his SUV. He promised to call Jack with the new location as soon as they got settled, and not to call anyone else. Jack still had nagging suspicions about Ralph Graham, but their happiness at seeing each other again seemed real. He said goodbye and drove the BMW back to his cottage. He called Detective Guthrie to give him an update on the Grahams and to ask for a protective detail around their mansion. Guthrie agreed and said people were already there.

CHAPTER 12:

SECOND DETECTIVE MEETING

Three days after the Graham yacht fire, the detective team met again in the Sheriff substation at Lucerne Ave. and the FEC railroad line. Jack Price had picked up Anna from her sailboat in his black BMW about 9:30, so they could get their own coffee and still make the 10:00 am meeting. Again, they parked in the small parking lot near the railroad line and entered the reception area. This time, Jack showed his reserve FBI detective credentials, and they both were ushered to the elevator. On the second floor, there were more people working, and the conference room was crowded. Updates had been marked and pictures added to the large white board at the end of the conference room.

Detective Guthrie came in with Sargeant Evans. When everyone was seated at the old metal conference table, Guthrie welcomed them and gave a quick update. "We have taken statements from all of the party goers that were on the yacht that night. We definitely have witnesses that saw two tall men dressed in black come on the boat about midnight.

They evidently shot the waiter and threw the Molotov cocktail that started the fire. Thanks to Anna Henderson, we also have found Mrs. Phyllis Graham alive, and she is now in seclusion with her husband. She evidently was able to escape the fire and stayed on a neighboring boat. On a sadder note, we have identified the dead woman as Melissa McKinley. She was the wife of a lawyer that worked in Mr. Guthrie's law firm and died from smoke inhalation. That is all I have. Let's go around the table and provide updates in each of your areas".

Sargeant Evans stated that they had interviewed 35 witnesses that were at the party at the time of the fire. Five of the witnesses saw two masked men in dark clothing come onto the yacht. One shot the waiter and the other threw the molotov cocktail in to the main salon. The time was approximately midnight. They saw the men run back down the stairs to the dock, but did not see where they went in the crowd of people running from the yacht. Several of the witnesses reported hearing screams after the fire started.

Anna reported on finding Mrs. Graham and her previous modeling career in New York City. Mrs. Graham lived in New York City and was a well-known model, working for several ad agencies, and fashion designers. She was well liked by her peers and appeared in many fashion magazines. Her agent provided a list of clients over the last five years, and they were all legitimate. Two years ago, she met

Mr. Graham, married him quickly and moved to Florida. I am still looking into her whereabouts prior to moving to New York.

Jack reported on his contacts with the FBI and Interpol. "We are looking into any connections that Mr. or Mrs. Graham might have had with criminal elements either in this country or in Europe. Mr. Graham has a long client list and may have enemies from his legal cases. Mrs. Graham's background before she came to New York is currently unknown. We are continuing to work with these agencies."

Guthrie added Mr. McKinley to the list of suspects, and reduced a few suspects that had strong alibis. Jack said, "At this point Mr. Graham is still a strong suspect. We need more information about his clients, and how he makes his money. Does he have ties to the mafia for money laundering, or has he used his boat for drug trafficking during trips to the Bahamas? We need to interview the yacht crew more closely".

Guthrie thanked the group, and said there would be another update in two days. They all trooped out of the conference room, and Jack yawned slightly. "Not much new information that we didn't provide. Hopefully, the case will break soon."

That afternoon Jack spent time on the computer checking out Mrs. Graham and her parents. He also called an old contact with the Polish intelligence service that he knew from his FBI days. "I need a favor. Can you find out anything about this model and her family? Her father is a professor at the university." "I can check to see if she has a record in Interpol or any known contacts with criminals. You haven't given me much to go on". "I know, but I am looking for any reason someone might want her killed."

CHAPTER 13:

PHYLLIS'S BACKGROUND

Jack Price was in his office on his third cup of coffee. The office was on the second floor of a commercial building at the corner of Lake Avenue and J Street across from the Lake Worth Playhouse. The office was four small rooms, consisting of a reception desk (currently vacant), offices for Jack and Anna, and a small conference room with a metal table and six chairs. The furnishings were spartan and his door had a painted sign saying Price Private Investigations.

The conference room had papers everywhere. Behind the metal table, a large cork board held pictures of the victims and murder suspects. The problem was that there were too many suspects. Motives for killing someone married to a lawyer were coming from all sides. It was like tossing a match into gasoline. You didn't know where it would spread.

His cell phone on the conference table rang and he picked it up. "Price Investigations he said by habit". "Hope I didn't call too early for you, said a European voice over the phone. I am about ready to call it a day". "Yes, you guys are 7 hours ahead of us in Poland". Did you find anything on the Graham woman? Jack had called a friend he knew in Interpol from his days in the FBI to check on Phyllis Graham and her background. "I checked and she does not have a record with Interpol or the Polish authorities. I also checked news stories while she was here. She was quite a sensation as a young model and traveled all over Europe. She had contact with many rich playboys and high-powered politicians. Of course, there were rumors about scandals, but none were proven. Perhaps, that is one reason she left for the US". Jack asked, "Do you have a list of names of the people she knew?" "Yes, and I will send it along with some newspaper clips. I will also send what I found out about relatives, parents and professors at the University. Her sister is married and lived in Donetsk until she was forced to leave by the war in Ukraine. Her uncle is a general in the Ukraine Army. He was a colonel then, but now he is in charge of the war effort with Russia. He does not have a family and loves his nieces. When they were growing up, he often visited and brought them expensive gifts". "Do you really think the Russians would come after her?" "They have a history of retaliation and a long reach. Look at the men poisoned in England". "Well, thanks for the information. I will add it to the list of

59

murder suspects that I have here. I wish I could cross some off instead of adding to them."

Jack went back into his office and pulled a bottle from his desk drawer. He poured a healthy slug into his coffee cup, and then sat down at the desk. He thought about the various suspects and the potential motives for the fire and murders. He still thought the main suspects were either Ralph Graham himself, or one of Ralph's clients that he had crossed. He was concerned about the safety of Phyllis with Ralph, but he had no proof of Ralph's guilt. And if Ralph was guilty, why was he hiring Jack to keep them safe? Jack had asked Anna to keep watch over the couple in their hide-away. So far, there had not been any other attacks.

Several miles away, three men were talking on the balcony of a different mansion. "How did you miss the woman?" a guttural voice snarled. "Our friends will not be happy with us." "I saw the woman go into the main salon, and the fire should have trapped her like it trapped and killed the other woman." "You weren't paid to kill the other woman. Have you found where they are hiding the Graham woman?" No, the papers still say there were two women killed, but that is not what my contact says at the morgue." "Find her and kill both her and the husband. We don't want any loose ends."

CHAPTER 14:
GRAHAM MEETING

Palm Beach County detective Guthrie and Jack Price walked up the drive to the West Palm Beach condo where the Grahams were staying. The condo was in a 20-story high-rise building in downtown West Palm Beach that was owned by a client of Mr. Graham. They went up the elevator and knocked at the door. Anna answered. She was staying at the condo for the Graham's protection. She put her pistol back in the holster behind her back, and led the way to where the Grahams were sitting on the sofa. "Thanks for seeing us", said Detective Guthrie. "Have you thought of anything new or anyone that seriously wants to harm you?" Mr. Graham answered, "I have many old and new cases. Most have large money implications. My office has made them available to you". "What about the most recent case? $100,000 is enough of a motive for murder". "These are big firms, and that kind of lawsuit is just a write off. There was a personal injury case about 6 months ago with a $500,000 award of damages. The homeowner on Palm Beach didn't have that kind of insurance and lost his house.

He definitely blames me. I'll have my secretary send you that file."

"What about you, Mrs. Graham? How long have you been married? What did you do before that?" "My life is an open book. I grew up in Ukraine. My parents were teachers at the University. I started out in college but got into modeling in Europe. Then I had a chance to come to New York City for a big show. I met Ralph in the hotel after the show and the rest is history. I love it here, but I miss the excitement of modeling." "Can you give me your parents' names and address? Do they still live in Europe?" "Yes, I will write them down before you leave". "We are trying to keep your location secret. You have to help us by not using phones, computers or tablets while you are here. You also need to make sure you are not followed if you go out." "We will give you a new phone to order meals, but you can't call people you know, or they will find you. Anna will stay with you for your protection, and she can bring things that you need." Both Mr. and Mrs. Graham nodded their agreement. Jack smiled at Anna and asked how it was going. "They think I am a high paid waitress," said Anna. "I can hold my own against them or anyone else that shows up." Jack promised to call that night and they shook hands a few seconds longer than necessary. Jack could tell Anna was getting tired of guard duty.

As detective Guthrie and Jack left, they compared notes. Guthrie said, "I will dig into the legal files and get more background on the dead man and woman. One of them could have been the intended victim." Jack said, "I will check into Mrs. Graham to see if I can get more information on her parents and relatives. We still don't have much of a reason for the attack. You need to assign a deputy to protect the Grahams so that Anna can help with the investigation".

The next day Jack and Anna met for lunch at Murray's tavern in Lake Worth Beach. After the orders, Jack said, "We need to do a full background on Mrs. Graham. Here is a copy of the information she gave me about her parents. We know she worked for a modelling agency in New York City. Why don't you continue to focus on New York City and what she has done here in Lake Worth Beach. I will get back with my contacts in Europe and will follow up with them. We need to find a motive for these murders before someone else gets hurt." Anna said "okay, I will check with my friends to see if she is up to something here that she did not mention. I will also check out what she did in New York City. The modeling scene is close-knit, and I have several friends in New York City. I will also check with friends in the gay and lesbian communities here. Anna was close to many of them in the modeling industry."

CHAPTER 15:

GRAHAM LEGAL CASES AND CLIENTS

Detective Guthrie saw several boxes of legal files that had been delivered to the substation when he went back to his office. He called Sergeant Evans, "I want you to pick three sharp patrolmen and start wading through these files. If any look promising, look them over yourself and make notes for me. Then you can report your progress every morning." "Evans looked at the boxes of files and groaned, "Boss, I am not a legal eagle. This will take forever." "Then you had better start early and stay late. I want answers about potential clients or adversaries that might have a reason to kill Mr. or Mrs. Graham. Check on the case Mr. Graham mentioned, where the adversary lost their house because they could not pay the damages. That is motive for murder to me. Get the man's name, find where he lives now and bring him in for questioning." Over the next four days, Evans and his team went through the boxes of legal files from Mr. Graham's office. Evans reported every morning and Guthrie picked the following cases to interview suspects.

Case One was Mr. Bunting. He had been in a car accident that had killed a teenager due to his drunk driving. Mr. Bunting was charged with DUI and manslaughter. The boy's family had sued for damages and been awarded $1.5 million. Mr. Bunting had been released after a five-year sentence, been divorced and had to sell his house to pay the damages. When Bunting was brought in, Guthrie began the questions. "Where were you last Friday night?" "I was working at a warehouse job on the afternoon shift from 3:00 to 11:00 pm. I got something to eat at the local diner and then went home to bed." "Did you have contact with Mr. Graham after the lawsuit?" "'No, I hated him because of the way he told the jury that I had murdered the boy, but I haven't seen him since then." "Do you know anyone that could have attacked the Grahams?" "No, there were guys in the prison that might do something" like that, but I didn't have anything to do with them." "Don't leave the area. We will check your alibi and may have further questions. Are you on parole?" "Yes, my parole officer can reach me."

Case Two was an import-export business that Mr. Graham had set up and helped manage for offshore clients that used banks in the Bahamas to cloak their identity. Graham had charged huge fees which were paid through offshore accounts. Guthrie reviewed this case, and asked Jack to have the FBI investigate further. "This whole thing looks shady." Jack contacted the FBI to see if they had a file on Graham or the import-export business. They reported that there was a file, but it had been closed due to a lack of evidence. Jack asked for a copy of the file.

Case Three was a corporate lawsuit, where one large company was suing another for patent infringement. The court awarded the first company $50 million dollars in damages and ruled that the other company had to stop marketing their high technology product. This case was being appealed, but it would bankrupt several millionaires if it was upheld. That much money was motive for murder. Both companies had lawyers, and Frank could not get a warrant for search warrants without further evidence.

Mr. Buntings alibi checked out, and Frank kept both case two and three for further investigation and as potential motives.

CHAPTER 16:

MELISSA MCKINLEY

The next day, Detective Guthrie received the coroner's report. It identified the male waiter from dental records and ruled his death a homicide due to a single shot in the head with a 9mm pistol. It identified the female victim from her dental records as Melissa McKinley. Death was due to smoke inhalation. These formal findings seemed sterile and did not indicate that two families had been devastated and would never be the same. Frank hated notifying the next of kin more than any other aspect of the detective job, but he knew it must be done. He ordered Sergeant Evans to make the notification for the waiter's family and drove out to notify Mr. McKinley. He called Ralph Graham's office and learned that Mr. McKinley was there, so he drove up Federal Highway from Lake Worth Beach to downtown West Palm Beach. He parked in a downtown parking garage and walked to the high rise building near the intracoastal. He knew that the McKinley's had two children, and thought about how this news would affect them. He showed his credentials to the law firm receptionist, and asked directions to McKinley's office. He knocked on the door and received a terse "Come In". As he entered, Mr. McKinley rose from his desk, recognized him from the yacht fire, and said, "Oh my God, No." His face was ashen as they stood there. Finally, he motioned for Guthrie to take a seat, and he collapsed into his desk chair. Frank began, "We received final confirmation from the coroner today that the female victim in the yacht fire last week was Mrs. McKinley. I am so sorry for your loss. Is there anyone you would like to call to be with you or the children during this terrible time?" Mr. McKinley covered his face with his hands for a minute, and then seemed to recover the ability to speak. "No, I already have my sister staying at the house to take care of the kids, and I was afraid this was the news that was coming." Guthrie said," I know this is a terrible time, but are you able to give me any other possibilities of anyone that might want to hurt your wife." "No, as I said before, she was well liked by everyone, and did not interact with the clients." "I know this is difficult, but we have heard that you and your wife were arguing that night on the yacht. What was that about?" "It was nothing, Melissa thought that I was spending too much time with clients and not enough time with her. She was drinking heavily because of that, and I thought she would embarrass us more. She went down to a berth to sleep it off. I wish I had taken her home instead. I will have to live with that the rest of my life." He covered his face again and waved Guthrie away. As Guthrie closed the office door, he could hear gentle sobs.

Detective Guthrie felt badly for Mr. McKinley, but he also had a job to do. When he got back to the substation, he added McKinley to the list of suspects. He asked Evans to get a warrant for his cell phone, computer and financial records. If there was another woman, the story could be different than what it appeared to be.

CHAPTER 17:

COMMISSIONER PETERS

Commissioner Peters and several friends were having drinks at Chuck's Last Call bar on Lake Avenue In downtown Lake Worth Beach Saturday evening. Chuck's was a combination open air bar and restaurant across the street from Murray's. The bar had cypress wood exterior, with sliding doors that rolled back so that the interior was open to the sidewalk. Tables and chairs were spread along the sidewalk and inside the restaurant so that patrons could sit inside or outside. A large mahogany bar with a mirror and liquor bottles was located along one side of the dining room, and stools were strung along the bar for those wanting a drink. Music played from a juke box so that it was heard both in the restaurant and on t6he street. Chuck's was known as a gathering place to meet friends, enjoy drinks and have a good meal. The restaurant was full and there was a lot of chatter and laughing.

It was a busy night with many people, cars and motorcycles in the downtown area. Commissioner Peters was celebrating his recent election victory with several friends and discussing environmental changes he wanted to make in Lake Worth Beach. He was sitting at a table on the street.

A loud motorcycle was stopped at the light beside Chuck's. It rumbled loudly as the driver revved the engine. Both the driver and rider were dressed in black with black helmets. The rider held a silenced 9mm Makarov pistol between him and the driver so only the barrel was sticking out. As the red light changed, the driver revved the engine and the motorcycle raced away from Chuck's bar. No one heard the soft discharge from the pistol. Suddenly, Peters slumped in his chair and dropped his drink. His friends crowded around him and saw a small red circle on his chest. As they watched the blood flow increase, people screamed and ran from the bar into the street. Someone called 911. Soon two sheriff Explorers came from the substation three blocks away and blocked the street. The deputies quickly called for an ambulance, taped off the scene and called in for backup.

Detective Guthrie groaned as his cell phone rang just as he was starting to have dinner with his wife. The dispatcher said, "911 call from Chuck's Last Call. Uniforms say there was a shooting". "I will be there. Why can't killers kill people during working hours?"

Jack Price and Anna were having dinner on the sidewalk at Murray's after a long day in the office.

A commotion started across the street at Chuck's Last Call. Two sheriff's deputies pulled to the curb with lights flashing. Jack took a long pull on his bourbon and got up to see what was going on. As he crossed the street, screaming people started leaving Chuck's restaurant. The deputy shouted, "Everyone move outside and give us some room." A woman at the first table near the entrance was crying and holding a man on the floor. Jack saw the bartender and asked what had happened. "A guy and his friends were having drinks at a table on the sidewalk. Suddenly, he fell. The whole group of people started screaming. Then this Deputy showed up". By that time, the sheriff supervisor and the ambulance were pulling up.

Jack went back to Murray's to tell Anna about the shooting and finished his meal. He and Anna watched the familiar routine taping off the scene and taking people's statements. After he finished his meal, he saw Sergeant Evans coming out to his car and he waved for him to come over. "What happened Al? Lake Worth Beach is pretty busy for a weekend." It was Commissioner Peters that was shot. We can't get a straight story from any of the witnesses. Most were drunk". Jack said, "Commissioner Peters was just elected. I didn't think anyone in Lake Worth Beach wanted to kill him." "Stay out of it Jack. Let us get to the bottom of it."

Jack and Anna watched as the deputies secured the crime scene, took statements from witnesses, and ushered in the coroner to perform his evaluation. They saw Detective Guthrie drive up to the scene, talk to Sergeant Evans and ask questions of the coroner. By that time, the deputies ordered everyone to clear the street. Jack and Anna walked back to the BMW in the rear parking lot behind Murray's. As they got into the car, Jack said, "Three murders in two weeks. And one was a commissioner. This is going to be all over the media. I wonder if there is any connection between the two cases." Anna replied, "They don't seem to have anything in common, but the media will be making up reasons to link them. I hope this doesn't become a circus."

Jack drove Anna home to the marina and watched her walk toward the dock. He couldn't help watching until she was out of sight. He shook his head and drove home to the green bungalow.

Later that night, the assassin made a call to report. "The problem has been solved and the cycle will not be found" he said. The guttural voice replied, "I heard on the news, Perhaps, the two of you are useful after all" "Find somewhere to lay low until things cool down. Don't come back here." "I understand," said the assassin, and ended the call. He turned and said to his partner, "Let's go to Miami for a few days."

73

CHAPTER 18:

FIRST TASK FORCE MEETING AND PRESS CONFERENCE

The morning after Commissioner Peters was shot, Jack woke to his cell phone ringing. "Price here he answered groggily". "You better wake up quick", said Detective Guthrie. "You and Anna need to get to City Hall by 10:00 am for an emergency Task Force meeting with all hands. Shooting a Commissioner has caused a firestorm in the Sheriff Department and at City Hall. The Sheriff will be at the meeting and at the Press Conference on the City Hall steps at noon. The Mayor will also be at the Press Conference, and we are being questioned about a serial killer". Jack was wide awake now. That kind of press could take all of the logic from an investigation, and just pin the killings on the first available loser. "We'll be there", he said.

He called Anna with the update and asked her to drive separately, and get the coffee, so that he could look over their notes. He showered and dressed in record time. The drive to City Hall was only five minutes in his BMW, but he wanted to be there ten minutes early. By the time he pulled into the parking lot, it was crowded with Sheriff SUVs, plainclothes sedans, and a SWAT vehicle. The normal city employees were not there, since it was a Saturday morning. The City Hall was closed to the public and the media. He parked and walked up the front steps.

The City Hall is a three-story structure located between Lake and Lucerne Avenue and fronting on Federal Highway. At one time the third floor was an auditorium, that seated up to 350 people. It was built in 1935 as the first fireproof building and as a hurricane shelter. The structure housed the Lake Worth Playhouse in the 1950s until they moved to a new theater. The structure was eventually remodeled as a City Hall with offices. It still functions as the City Hall for Commission meetings and houses the City Manager and Clerk.

The City Hall Conference Room is on the second floor, adjacent to the Commission meeting room. It is a large conference room with a mahogany table, padded wooden armchairs, and a dozen extra chairs at the back of the room. A large whiteboard had been added for the task force meeting, with pictures of both the victims and suspects.

There were several new faces when Jack walked into the meeting. The Palm Beach County

Sheriff was sitting at the center of the conference table, already holding court. The Sherrif was responsible for the safety of over 1.5 million people in the county and was one of the most powerful people in county politics. The Captain for Lake Worth Beach was on his right and Detective Guthrie was on his left. Both knew this could be a career maker or breaker, depending on what happened in the next few days. Guthrie introduced Jack as a liaison with the FBI. In addition, there was a liaison with the Florida Department of Law Enforcement, the Coroner's Office, the City Manager, and the Attorney General's office. All the bases were covered.

Jack took a seat at the end of the conference table, and Anna came in and wisely took a seat in the back. At 10:00 am sharp, the Sheriff called for order, and started the meeting. "The shooting of a newly elected Commissioner is an attack on the very fabric of government in our country, and I will not rest until we find the culprit and bring them to justice. I have established a task force this morning with all law enforcement agencies involved, so we can quickly bring these criminals to justice. All avenues of investigation will be followed and all of the department's resources will be available to find these killers. Detective Guthrie will continue to lead this task force, and will coordinate with all of the agencies. I want full cooperation on all sides. Now, Detective, please bring us all up to speed on where we stand".

Detective Guthrie, looking more haggard than usual, stood. "Commissioner Peters was shot in Chuck's Last Call on Lake Avenue about 8:00 pm last night. Deputies flooded the area within five minutes of the shots, secured the crime scene and took statements from the witnesses. The Coroner declared Commissioner Peters dead at the site, with one gunshot wound to the chest. There will be an autopsy later today. Several witnesses reported two men dressed in black, with black helmets, on a loud motorcycle at the red light next to the restaurant. At least one witness reported seeing one of the men raise a pistol and shoot the Commissioner before leaving the scene. We have put out an APB on the motorcycle, and checked CCTV in the area, but have not found the motorcycle yet. We have issued warrants for all phone, email and financial records from the City Manager, City Commissioners, and the previous Commissioner that lost the election to Mr. Peters. We will be taking statements from all of these people and checking alibis. We are also investigating large business interests that have had issues come up recently, or issues scheduled for the near future. The task force will meet every morning in this conference room at 9:00 am. We will be following up all leads".

The City Manager thanked the Sherrif and said that he and the entire city staff were in shock at the vicious murder of a commissioner in Lake Worth. He assured all parties that the City would cooperate fully with the investigation and would help in any way they could to fine the murderers. Flags will be flown at half-staff for thirty days in remembrance of Commissioner Peters. "I have talked with Mrs. Peters and we will be assisting the family as much as we can."

He also announced that all controversial policy issues would be delayed until a full City Commission was available to hear them. "This is meant to assure the citizens that we are not rushing controversial items through during the investigation."

When the meeting had wound down, everyone took a quick break until the Press Release started at noon. The Press Release was a staged event for both TV and written media. There were six TV trucks broadcasting live feeds for the noon news cycle, and thirty reporters standing at the bottom of the City Hall steps. At the appointed time, the Sheriff, City Mayor and District Attorney took the lead in expressing outrage that a City Commissioner had been shot, and assuring the public that the case would receive the highest priority in the County. Detective Guthrie was announced as the leader of the task force, and asked the public for any information that might be helpful to the case. Everyone related to the case shuddered at how much work that statement would generate. Once the statements were completed, all of the reporters began screaming their questions. One that rang out above the rest was quickly taken up by other reporters, so that it had to be answered. As usual, the difficult questions were given to Guthrie.

"Are there Assassins here in Lake Worth Beach?" Guthrie said, "We are investigating every possibility," but he knew that every news organization would use that question as their lead story.

CHAPTER 19:

SECOND TASK FORCE MEETING

Detective Guthrie opened the second Task Force Meeting the next day at 9:00 am, Sunday, at the City Hall conference Room. This was going to be a long working meeting. He updated everyone on the progress of the case to date and then gave assignments for the coming days.

"The Sheriff headquarters building has set up a hot line to take calls regarding the three murder cases. We have pulled in 20 patrolmen and 3 detectives to review and follow up on these calls. So far, there have already been 220 calls, and we expect many more over the next few days. Any legitimate leads will be sent to this task force. I have established a large war room in the substation, and we have five extra people to coordinate and report information, so make sure to write progress reports by 6:00 pm every day."

"I am asking the FBI to investigate any of Mr. Graham's legal cases that could be related to persons with drug or mafia connections. These cases appear to be much more lucrative than they should be."

"Mr. Price will be investigating foreign ties with this case through his contacts with Interpol, and Miss Henderson will be investigating Mrs. Graham's connections to the modeling world here and in New York."

"I am asking the FDLE to investigate all of the Commissioners, the City Manager, city staff and any large developers or contractors that have been or will soon be doing business with the City. They can request assistance from any of the City departments."

"The Sheriff's office will continue to follow any and all leads related to the gunmen and the motorcycle used in the Peters murder."

"I know these are huge assignments in addition to your normal workload. This is the highest priority now. Put your other work aside and get this done."

As the task force meeting broke up, Jack stepped over to Guthrie with a mock salute and said "Yavo my commandant." Guthrie smiled and said, "Did I lay it on too thick." "No, but don't try that speech with your wife." They walked out the double doors of City Hall and down the stairs to their cars.

CHAPTER 20:

SEMINOLES

Cameron loved the Seminole Hotel casino. It was a glittering 20 story hotel shaped like an electronic guitar, with lights that could be seen for 20 miles. The hotel was 400 feet tall and housed 500 luxury suites with floor to ceiling windows that gave a stunning view of South Florida. The hotel lobby had gold-colored furnishings and white marble floors. A huge pool with cabanas and bars made guests think they were in Tahiti. The hotel lobby connected directly to the casino, which had beautifully appointed rooms for slot machines, black jack, roulette and poker. Dining and shows provided entertainment breaks between gambling. It was owned by the Seminole Indian tribe, and known for first class entertainment, dining and high stakes gambling. He could Indulge all of his vices in one place when he came here.

Tonight, he was here for business instead of pleasure. Cameron was dressed in a $2000 suit with alligator boots, a Rolex watch and a diamond ring. He looked the part of a successful South Florida developer. He had sold many projects in similar meetings, but tonight was important to him. He needed this project to go forward.

Having a casino approved in Florida was only possible if you kissed the ring of the Seminole Indians. Today, he was meeting an attorney from the tribe. They met in a lavish conference room above the gaming tables. Here, things were all business. Everyone greeted each other, were served coffee or tea, and took seats at the large table. Cameron would have liked something stronger and thought that he would stop for a drink after the meeting. "This is a beautiful place you have here." "Not too shabby for a reservation, right?" Cameron smiled and began his pitch.

"I have several sites that would be good to expand your casino business in Florida. You are already doing well, and I can help you make a lot more money. I would be happy to show them to you, and discuss a development plan that is mutually beneficial". The lawyer was quiet for a moment, "How do you think we got casinos in Florida. They all are on Tribal Indian Land. The land must be on a reservation or owned by Seminole Indians. They all must be governed and owned by the Seminole tribe. We can't do anything that would jeopardize our birthright".

Cameron answered, "I wouldn't consider breaking those legal requirements, but you must have some flexibility if it helps you expand and make more money for the tribe" "Any additional land would have to show a direct tie to the Seminole Indians and make a claim that the land was in fact tribal land. The Seminoles ranged all over Florida prior to the Civil War, but there are not many known cases of Seminole land ownership outside the reservations". "I will check the ownership history of the sites that I have in mind. Seminoles did live throughout Florida at one time. I don't think it will be a problem if we make the right case to the right people. I can give them a powerful incentive to work with us." "The idea of a development partnership may be possible, if the tribe maintains ownership and control of the casinos. There are many ways to structure a deal, and we can talk further about them in future, if you have a lucrative site."

"Thank you for your time, and for the information. I will let you know when I have the information you are requesting, so that we can move forward"

Cameron took the elevator to the gaming floor, walked over to the bar, and ordered a double scotch. This project was going to be more difficult than he had thought. He needed to show that there was a connection between the Lake Worth pool site and the Seminoles. And he needed the approval from the Lake Worth Commission. A new commissioner could give him the three vote majority he needed, but it would be expensive and risky to elect a ringer to do his bidding, He also had a time frame to show progress on this project. He couldn't wait until the heat died down to get it done. His partner was powerful and dangerous. He had to get this project off the ground.

He finished his drink at the bar and eyed the casino. Maybe he could salvage the evening at the tables.

CHAPTER 21:

COMMISSIONER MEETING

It was the first commissioner meeting after Commissioner Peters was shot. City Manager Mobley was talking with the remaining commissioners before the meeting. "I know this meeting will be tough. People are outraged that Commissioner Peters was shot. They feel like their election was stolen. I do not think it is a good time to bring up any major policy issues, especially the possible sale of the pool. Since there are only four seated commissioners, I need three votes to proceed with any action. Two votes will be considered a negative vote. Therefore, if you are not sure you have three votes, I recommend you continue the discussion until a later meeting". There was grumbling from all the commissioners about this situation. "How can we get anything done while we have four commissioners? Can we appoint a fifth commissioner to the vacancy until a special election? "Mobley said," the Governor is the only person that can appoint a commissioner. I don't think you would like his pick. I suggest instructing the City Attorney to begin work to expedite a special election to fill the vacant Commissioner seat. In the meantime, we will handle the normal business of the city. Are you ready to start the meeting?" The commissioners, City Attorney and City Manager left the City Manager's office and filed into their places in the Commission room.

The Lake Worth Beach city hall was a historic building that was over 100 years old, and badly needed to be refurbished. Restrooms were crumbling, plumbing was breaking, and the air conditioning was questionable. The commission meeting room was on the second floor, served by an ancient two-person elevator. The commissioner's raised walnut desk was at one end of the room, and the public filed in at the back of the room. There was seating for about sixty people, and often, the staff had to wait in an adjacent conference room to be called to speak.

The commissioners came in and sat at their raised desks along with the city manager and the contracted city attorney. The commission room was already packed with people and newspaper reporters. The people were rowdy and were already talking about Commissioner Peters. "You can't trust any of them." The reporters were asking leading questions and insinuating that the Commissioners might be involved in the murder. "Did you know that three Commissioners have run this town for years?" "Did you know that they want to sell the pool again?" The City Manager raised his hands and called for quiet. "Just settle down, you will get your chance to talk during the public comments."

The mayor called for order and started the meeting with the Pledge of Allegiance. After some preliminary routine items, the new business was considered. The second item on the agenda was to consider ways to increase revenue from the pool and casino building. The city manager gave a short presentation on the low revenue. "The pool and casino building continue to be losers in the budget. We have made improvements to the operations, but it is not enough. This money has to be made by other departments and increases taxes and fees on citizens. It has been suggested that we look for proposals from the private sector to increase this revenue and balance the budget." The crowd went wild with catcalls, whistles and shouts about rotten politics. The mayor banged her gavel, and the crowd eventually quieted.

Commissioner Nichols stated that the best way to increase revenue was to ask the private sector for proposals. Two other commissioners disagreed and said that private proposals had been tried before. None were acceptable. Following rancorous discussion by the commissioners, input was requested from the public. A long list of people came to the podium, and almost all of them disagreed with closing the pool. "I grew up here and love the pool. As a kid, I went with other kids to enjoy the pool during hot summer days. I want kids now to have that same experience. We need to get the pool back open." "We don't know who we can trust in the city until the Sheriff completes his investigation into the murder of Commissioner Peters." "I think it's time to throw all of you out and start over with a new City Commission." "Don't do anything that will raise my taxes. I barely get by as it is."

The city manager saw that there was no way to obtain a majority. He therefore asked to continue this item to a future agenda. After more arguments, the Mayor asked for a vote to continue this item. Mr. Cameron was sitting at the back of the commission meeting. He got up and walked out. "I don't know if these buffoons will ever make a decision."

CHAPTER 22:

THIRD TASK FORCE MEETING

Three days after Commissioner Peters was shot, the Task Force met again in a closed meeting at the City Hall Conference Room. People took their normal places around the big mahogany table, and in the metal seats in back. Detective Guthrie was in charge, and neither the Sheriff nor the City Manager attended. A few reporters tried to get statements as people trooped into City Hall, but they were not rewarded with any scoops.

Detective Guthrie started the meeting, after a preliminary welcome. "The Coroner's report on Commissioner Peters confirmed that he was killed by one bullet to the chest. We have been able to compare the bullet taken from the waiter at the Graham house, with the bullet taken from Commissioner Peters. They came from the same gun, so we know the same two men were involved in both crimes. We are now trying to make a connection between Mr. Graham and Commissioner Peters. Why would someone use the same two assassins to attack the Grahams and kill

Commissioner Peters? They clearly did not have the same social circle or business ties. As far as we know, Mr. Graham did not have any clients with issues before the City Commission. We finally found the motorcycle used in the murder. It was stolen and was found burned in a remote part of John Prince Park, just west of Lake Worth Beach. There were no prints, DNA or CCTV results found."

Jack continued, "I have been making contact with the FBI, DEA and Homeland Security. You all are familiar with the Muslim extremists that were trained at Lantana Airport, just 3 miles from here. We have not found any links like that yet, but we have found ties from Mr. Graham's firm to both Mafia underworld and drug clients. That is one reason Mr. Graham is so wealthy. When his phone and financials were investigated, it is clear that he has set up dummy corporations for both types of clients, and may have been involved more directly. If he was skimming money from these guys, they would not hesitate to hire hitmen to kill him. We are also investigating a potential insurance fraud to burn the yacht and recover cash".

Detective Guthrie said "that may explain the Graham case, but it does nothing to explain the tie between Graham and Peters. Where are we with checking the phone calls and emails of the Commissioners to check for suspicious ties?" The FDLE liaison spoke up, "We received a warrant, and pulled all the phone and email records for the Commissioners, City Manager and Building Official. We are still going through them, but they were clearly all involved with developers or business owners as part of their duties. We haven't found a "smoking gun" yet". "Well, keep at it", replied Guthrie. "Let's focus on the big development proposed for the beach that was just defeated last night. The timing of the shooting and the Commission meeting makes that development suspect."

After additional reports and comments, Detective Guthrie closed the meeting, and they all trooped out of the City Hall. Jack asked Anna to see if she could find anything more about the developer of the pool-hotel project.

CHAPTER 23:
DEVELOPER AND HISTORIAN MEETING

The Palm Beach County Historical Society was located in the old county courthouse that had been completely renovated. It was located beside the new County Administration Building just west of S Olive Street. The Palm Beach County Courthouse was built in 1916 in a neo-classical design with a large three-story porch entrance with Greek columns supporting the porch. It had three stories and originally held all the county offices. Now it housed the historical society and many historical exhibits.

Cameron pulled his Mercedes into a parking space in the lot across from the administration building and walked to the old courthouse. He walked into the building and asked for the historian on duty. A retired man came to the desk. "Hello, I am James Cameron". "I am Phillip Summers, said the man, what can I do for you?"

"I am interested in learning about land that was owned by the Seminole Indians", Cameron said.

Summers said, "There are maps showing the Seminole Indian reservations, both now and in the past. Would that be helpful?" "Yes, please make me a copy of those. Are there any other ways that Seminole Indians could have owned land?" "The Seminole Indian tribe was a diverse mix of Indians forced off their original lands, slaves hiding from capture, and criminals that were running from prison. They lived in many areas of what was then Monroe County. Many lived in swampy areas and made no claims on the land. Other old claims were never recorded or were lost. I can check, if any of the old land claims included a Seminole Indian owner. These claims were made in Key West and many of the claims were lost during fires that occurred in Key West". "Please see what you can find. Send them to my office. Here is a card with my contact information". Cameron said goodbye, left the building and went back to his car. He was not very hopeful that he would find anything useful.

A week later, his secretary sauntered into the office with an email from the historian. He read, "I was able to find some information on Seminole land ownership in the 1800's. There were two areas in Palm Beach County that were shown. One was near Jupiter at the site of the State Park where Seminole Indians fought Union soldiers in the Seminole Wars. The other site was located on what is now Palm Beach Island. There is a book about the "barefoot mailman" that provided mail service from Miami to Palm Beach. One chapter talked about him finding a Seminole Indian living on the beach. The mailman helped the Indian make a claim for the land. The Indian's name was Aloysius James. He was a runaway slave from Georgia. I then checked land claim records from Key West. I did not find any claims that were related to this story. Many of those records were burned when Key West burned in 1900. I hope that information is helpful." Cameron turned to his secretary. "See if you can find any information about Aloysius James or the land claim on Palm Beach Island. That could be a diamond in the rough."

The next afternoon his secretary waltzed into the office. "I have some more information. I looked on Ancestry to see if I could find any information on Aloysius James. There was an old record in Georgia about a sale of land which also included a list of slaves in the early 1800s. It included Aloysius James. In 1820, there was a newspaper report of a slave runaway named James. It said they had looked for him with dogs but he went south into the swamps. Ancestry includes a death record for a Mr. James in 1870. He was buried in West Palm Beach. He had a wife and two sons. They still lived on Palm Beach Island. There is a sketchy trail from those sons to the present-day Pastor James Morris and his son Tom Morris. They are the last living relatives of this James. I printed out the ancestry documents for you and here is the file"

Cameron was amazed anyone was related to the Indian. It is very hard to believe this is real. If so, it may be what I am looking for and may be worth millions. Thank you for your efforts. Please keep this quiet and take the rest of the day off. If it works out, there will be a big bonus in your account". Cameron called Commissioner Nichols. "Have you ever heard of Pastor James Morris?" "Oh, yes. Pastor Morris leads a black church in District 1. He has been a pastor for at least 20 years and is well respected. His church is small and helps the homeless with food drives and clothes. Why do you want to know?" "His name came up when I was doing a land search", replied Cameron. "The only land that he owns is for his church and the small house next door. He is part of the black pastors that want to keep Lake Worth Beach like it has always been. He grew up here and came back to help the people living here. He has preached on the need to give Lake Worth kids more activities, including reopening the pool". "Would he change his mind for a very large donation to his church?" "I doubt it. I have tried on other issues." "I was afraid of that"

Cameron asked, "do you know his son Tom?" "Yes, he has drifted from one job to another. He drinks and has several minor scrapes with the law. He does not like his father and just wants to drift through life." "That is very interesting. I will have a talk with Tom James. Thanks for the information. I will call you later".

Cameron reached for a bottle in his desk drawer and poured two fingers into a glass. He sipped the scotch while he was thinking about his next step. Things were getting dicey, and he couldn't let this project get away. He made a decision, pulled out his encrypted cell phone and dialed a number by heart. "What do you want," asked a guttural voice. Cameron said, "just one more is what I need to bring this project through for you." The man snarled. "It had better happen for your sake. Give me the details." Cameron spelled out what was needed.

CHAPTER 24:

MCKINLEY INTERVIEW

The next day, the FBI Director of the WPB office and Jack Price marched into the legal offices of Mr. Graham. They first asked to see Mr. McKinley. When he came in, his eyes widened, and his heart rate went up when the FBI Director introduced himself. No one wanted the FBI to come after them. Jack started a recorder and began the questioning. "Mr. McKinley, state your full name and address." He did so. "Do you swear that you will tell the whole truth and nothing but the truth. Lying to federal officials is a felony punishable by prison time." Mr. McKinley answered shakily, "I do."

Jack continued," I am sorry for the loss of your wife. We need to ask you additional questions to try and solve her murder. These are procedural, and we are asking all potential witnesses these questions. Where were you the night of the yacht fire at midnight?" "I was on the upper deck of the yacht, talking to some existing clients. I have already given you their names." "Have you ever had any contact with gunmen for hire?" "When I was a junior district attorney, I did try a case of a gunman for hire. The gunman was found guilty and is in prison for life, but we could not find sufficient evidence to indict the man that hired the gunman." "Please give us the name and last address for this person. Did you recognize the two men that came onto the boat that night." "No, I told you this in my statement." Can you provide any further details about the men or about the shooting and fire that took place." "No." "Have you ever been threatened due to a case or a client?" "I have had a few minor threats during cases and have provided a list of those people already." "Are you having or have ever had an affair while you were married?" McKinley winced at the question. "I had a short affair with a secretary about three years ago, but I ended it and she moved to a different firm." We were happily married, and I loved my wife." Jack raised an eyebrow and asked for the women's name and current contact information.

The FBI Director then continued the interrogation. "Were you ever involved with legal cases for this firm involving drug or mafia related figures?" "No, I am a junior partner in the firm, and any of those cases were handled by the senior partner in the firm." "Did you know what was being done as part of those cases?" "No, I was not involved in them." "The fact that you are a partner in the firm makes you legally responsible for actions of the firm. You have just admitted that you knew or suspected that illegal actions were being taken by your firm. The fact that you did not report those suspicions makes you suspect. You could be an accessory to fraud, money laundering and possibly murder." McKinley's face was now white, and he was sweating heavily. "Look, I was not involved in any of those cases. If there was something done wrong, Mr. Graham was responsible for those clients. The cases were very lucrative, and he insisted on doing all of the legal work himself." "Did you see the people that met with Graham on these cases?" "No, but his secretary made the appointments and showed them into his office." "Mr. McKinley, we may need to talk with you again. Please do not leave the area without contacting my office first or discuss these matters with anyone. Here is my card."

CHAPTER 25:
GRAHAM INTERVIEW

Following the interview with Mr. McKinley and a short break to discuss strategy, they asked Mr. Graham to come to the conference room. By now everyone in the office knew that the FBI was investigating something related to the firm. There were discussions raging in corridors and closed offices. Finally, Mr. Graham came into the conference room, with another attorney. Jack introduced Mr. Graham and the FBI Director. They shook hands and sat down at the conference table, but the room felt frosty from the tension in the room. The FBI Director began, "As part of our investigation into the assassins that attacked your yacht and murdered two people, we have been looking at the clients and legal cases you have had. Most of these cases were normal commercial lawsuits or preparation of corporate documents. However, we have seen multiple cases involving personnel or firms that are known fronts for mafia operations and drug cartels. These cases involved setting up corporate fronts for their operations, helping to defraud the government through shady business contracts and money laundering. We know that the legal fees you charged were outrageous, and that those fees have contributed greatly to your wealth. We also suspect that you have outstanding tax issues related to these fees, and we can contact the IRS to investigate those issues separately. When and how did you get involved with these people?" Mr. Graham was not easily pressured, and he replied, "I don't know anything about these supposed claims you have made. I am the senior partner in the firm, and don't do day to day legal work anymore. If one of my associates has done something illegal, we will cooperate with you to find the guilty party." "Mr. Graham don't waste my time, we know you handled these accounts personally, and that you are responsible. I could arrest you right now with the evidence we have, but Mr. Price has suggested a different outcome. We know you have been attacked by one or more assassins. If you were put into the jail, how long do you think you would last?" Graham looked to his attorney wild-eyed and started sweating through his $500 shirt. "What do you have in mind?" The Director continued, "We are after the heads of these organizations. If you lead us to them and help to make sure they are convicted, we are willing to consider placing you and your wife in the witness protection program. Of course, you will have to give up the wealth related to these cases, but you will still be free to live your lives without looking over your shoulder." Graham sat back in his chair, stunned by the dramatic change in his fortunes.

"What would I have to do?" "Tell us everything, wear a wire to collect evidence and then testify against them. It won't be pleasant, but you will live." Graham conferred with his attorney for a few minutes. "I will do it," he said, "but you have to protect us from these assassins as well as the mob." They spent another hour discussing details and drafting a statement for Mr. Graham that admitted to his part in the crimes. He was then allowed to gather his coat and walk out of the office with them, rather than be put in handcuffs.

Jack called Guthrie after the meeting and updated him on this stunning development. "That is one part of the puzzle I didn't see coming," said Guthrie. "Did he give you any names of the people involved in these crimes? Could any of them have hired the assassins." Jack said, "The people that Graham has named are way up the ladder. I wouldn't be surprised if someone hired a killer. This opens up a whole new line of suspects in these murders." Guthrie said, "Great, all we need is some more suspects." Jack promised to provide more information once it was cleared by the FBI Director. This promised to be a big case, and he knew they would not want to release the names too soon.

CHAPTER 26:

TWO GUNMEN

Sergeant Evans and several patrolmen were tasked with identifying any past cases in Florida where two gunmen committed multiple crimes. They dug through electronic case files over the last fifteen years. They used both the Sheriff files and FDLE files for the entire state. Two gunmen working together was a fairly rare occurrence. They included cases of assault, robbery, and murder. After several days slogging through computer searches, Evans had assembled a list of 12 pairs of gunmen. Five of these were still in prison, two pairs were dead, three pairs had been released from prison and two pairs were still at large. He investigated the five pairs of gunmen that were currently free. One pair was in their sixties and not likely to be active. He contacted the parole officers of the two pairs still on parole, and learned that they had firm alibis for the dates of the murders. He put out an APB to arrest the last two pairs on suspicion of the murders. He also started contacting known associates, and searching previous addresses. It was a slow process, but he was hopeful that one of the pairs were the gunmen responsible for the murders.

One pair of gunmen were arrested in Broward County, just south of Palm Beach County. Sergeant Evans drove to the Broward County Jail. The Broward County Jail is an eight-story maximum security facility adjacent to the Broward County Courthouse in downtown Fort Lauderdale, approximately 40 miles south of Lake Worth. It was built in 1985 and expanded over the years to hold 1500 prisoners. Sergeant Evans had called ahead to make arrangements to interview the prisoners. He entered the main gate, showed his credentials, went through security and was met by a Broward sergeant that showed him to an interview room. He planned to interview the two gunmen separately. The first prisoner was brought into the interview room in cuffs. "How long have you been in Broward County?" "We just drove in from Tampa yesterday." "Who can confirm that you were in Tampa?" "We were staying with my sister for the last two weeks. She got tired of us, so we drove down here to stay with my aunt that lives in Fort Lauderdale." The gunman was forty-five, balding and had a sizable belly. He did not match the description given by either of the witnesses to the two murders. Evans took the addresses and phone numbers where the pair were staying. He then repeated the interview with the second prisoner and confirmed that the two statements were similar. He thanked the Broward sergeant and left. The two were being held on existing warrants for other cases. As Evans drove back to Lake Worth Beach on I-95, he did not think the two prisoners were involved in the Lake Worth murders. He was still hopeful that he would find the pair that matched the descriptions of his witnesses.

CHAPTER 27:

MEETING - PASTOR MORRIS

James Cameron, the wealthy hotel developer, was still angry about the last commission meeting. He had thought that with that new Commissioner Peters out of the way, the other three would fall into line behind Nichols and vote for the beach hotel. He grumbled to himself as he drank his third cup of coffee in his grand office in a West Palm Beach tower facing the intracoastal. He said, "I will make this happen, with or without that commission".

He grabbed the phone on his big walnut desk and dialed a number by heart. "Michael, I need you to meet with a black pastor, James Morris in Lake Worth Beach. I don't want to get involved directly. There is nothing illegal about the meeting, but I want to keep my name a secret for now. I will send over some background documents by courier. There is a rumor that this pastor may have a long lost relative that was a Seminole Indian. If so, I want to find out how long ago his relatives came here, and where they settled. Ask if he has any documents that would substantiate his family history. You can say that your client is researching stories about Seminole Indians to write a book.

The black lawyer, Mr. Michael Bellows, leaned back in his large desk chair, looked out his window to the intracoastal and thought, I have had many strange assignments in my career. When you work for rich people, they can ask strange questions. As long as it isn't illegal, it still pays very well. He dialed his secretary, asked her to make an appointment with Pastor Morris at his church, and asked her for any background on Pastor Morris.

A week later, Mr. Bellows drove his rental Ford SUV to the meeting with Pastor Morris. He didn't want to take a chance losing his new Mercedes in that neighborhood. He was dressed casually in chino slacks, a blue polo shirt and brown loafers. He also had left his Rolex watch in the office. He drove down US 1. Federal Highway, through West Palm Beach, through downtown Lake Worth Beach, and turned right on 12th Avenue S across the FEC railroad tracks. He went past the "friendship wall" that had separated whites and blacks during segregation. The site of that wall with paintings and graffiti made him wince to think that it still existed in the twenty-first century. He then turned left again at Wingfield Drive and drove almost to the end of the street, south of 15th Ave. S. The houses were small, with bars on the windows and flashy cars on the street. There were three small churches within two blocks. They were across the street from the rundown community park and community center. Bellows parked in front of the "Life of Hope" church, and walked up to the front door of the church. It was a one story stucco building with a sloped shingled roof, and a wooden cross on the top. He rang the electronic bell at the entrance, and heard a deep voice say, "come in". He opened the front wooden doors and went inside. It was cool and dark in the sanctuary. A middle-aged black man was coming out of a side door as he entered. "Come in, my name is Pastor James Morris. What can I do for you?" Pastor Morris was a tall strong man of about 50, with graying short hair, a gray suit and tie. His voice was deep and mellow.

"My name is Michael Bellows. I am an attorney in town, and am here doing some research for a client. Don't worry, there is nothing wrong and I don't want any money from the church. In fact, I am here to make a rather substantial donation for my client". He pulled out an envelope from a black case he was carrying, and gave it to Pastor Morris. The envelope contained a cashier's check for $1000. "Well, this donation will be extremely helpful for our small church. Will you come back to my office?" He led the way back to a small but cozy office with a wooden desk and two wooden chairs.

"My client is doing research on the early Seminole Indians in South Florida. He has an interest in writing a book to better describe their lives, struggles and achievements. Since the Seminoles covered such a large area of Florida, he has asked several attorneys to make preliminary inquiries. If there is a bigger story, he will then want to interview you further. If that is the case, there will also be additional donations. We are interested in an old historical rumor that a Seminole Indian lived in this area before the Civil War. Are you aware of any information about that subject? Would you mind if I recorded the interview so I can share it with him?"

Pastor Morris rocked back on the legs of his chair. "I haven't thought of that story for a long time. I grew up here in Lake Worth Beach. It was a struggle, but I had strong parents and a good teacher in elementary school. Back then, schools were still segregated. When I was a teen, I got into trouble, but was sent to juvenile court. That straightened me out. I went into the army and went to Vietnam. The things we saw there, I don't ever want to see again. Then I got out and used the GI bill to get an education. I got a job with the City Parks department, and now I supervise the Parks facility crews. I got married and raised a family. About twenty years ago, I looked at this community and knew it needed a place of Hope, love and forgiveness. I went to night school to become a pastor and opened a house church to serve the homeless, drug addicts and working people in the community. Now we have a congregation of 200 people. I still work my city job to make ends meet, and we struggle to pay the light bill. But we feed the hungry, shelter the homeless and give hope to those stuck in these streets. Jesus has led me into a better life here on earth".

"My family has been in this community for generations. My grandfather told me a story when he was old that his grandfather had told him. Our ancestor was a slave in Georgia before the Civil War. His master was brutal, and beat the slaves. He also broke up their families by selling them. One night, our ancestor escaped from the plantation. Somehow, he evaded the dogs and the men sent after him by going south into the big swamps. He almost died in those swamps, but was found by a group of Indians and former slaves. He joined them and learned how to live in the swamps. There were pine hammocks where they could make lean-tos and survive. Over time, he worked his way south into what is now Florida along the Suwannee River. He then kept moving south and east until he found the Atlantic Ocean that they called the Big Water. He used a dugout canoe to travel south in the lakes and streams near the ocean until he finally came to what is now Palm Beach Island. He settled there, because of the nice weather, the breezes and the abundant fishing. Over time, he took an Indian woman as his wife and had several children."

"Do you remember the man's name?", asked Bellows. "It was Aloyisus James. That is one reason my first name is James". "Did he ever make a claim for the property where he lived?" Pastor Morris continued, "It is hard for people to own property now, and it was much harder for a runaway slave at that time. But there was a white man that offered to help people claim their land, so that they couldn't be pushed off it. He was called the "Barefoot Mailman." They wrote a book about him. He and others walked the 60 miles along the beach from Miami to Palm Beach Island to deliver mail and news. Since Palm Beach was the end of his walk, he used to stay with Aloyisus to rest up before he returned. One time, he brought land claim forms from Key West and helped Aloyisus fill them out. You could claim 40 acres that was your homestead. He then took the forms back to Miami and sent them to Key West to be filed, along with many of the other settlers". "What became of those claims?," asked Bellows. "After several years, the barefoot mailman came back and gave Aloyisus a signed deed from the State of Florida. That deed has been a family heirloom ever since. It is hanging in a frame on my wall at home". "Was the land ever sold?" "No, eventually the white settlers and developers moved into the island. When they did, they took the land owned by the Indians or the blacks. We were forced off Palm Beach Island to West Palm Beach and then to the segregated portion of Lake Worth Beach. We have been there ever since."

Mr. Bellows said, "that is an extraordinary story and I am sure my client will want to talk with you. Would you ever be willing to part with that deed. It could be worth some money as a historical document." "Mr. Bellows, that deed was passed down for more than 150 years. I would never part with it". "I understand," said Bellows. Rising from the chair he shook hands and said thank you for taking the time to tell that amazing story. "I am sure we will be getting back with you soon".

As Mr. Bellows drove back to his office, he was amazed that a land claim from before the civil war was still being kept by a pastor.

CHAPTER 28:

FOURTH TASK FORCE MEETING

Detective Guthrie called another Task Force Meeting at City Hall to update everyone on developments and hear their status reports. The investigation was building momentum and he wanted to make sure it continued. People took their places around the large mahogany table and in the metal seats behind the conference table.

Detective Guthrie started the meeting. "I know that you have all been working hard, and we are making progress. We are not making any public statements yet because we are still gathering evidence, so all information is considered confidential. We have interviewed Mr. McKinley and Mr. Graham. Mr. McKinley is not a suspect in his wife's murder, and he has been cooperating in the investigation. Mr. Graham is involved in various crimes in relationship to clients with known drug and mafia ties. We are still investigating whether any of these clients could have contracted assassins to attack him and Mrs. Graham on their yacht."

Sergeant Evans reported, "We have been investigating any known cases where two gunmen worked together. We have narrowed the field and have arrested one pair in Fort Lauderdale. It appears that they are not the ones that attacked here, but they are in custody for other crimes. We still have one outstanding arrest warrant and are hoping for action on that case."

The FDLE liaison reported, "We have identified the developer involved in the recent attempt to buy the Lake Worth pool site on the beach and convert it to a large-scale hotel and casino. The developer is James Cameron, and he has an office in West Palm Beach. We are waiting for warrants to search his home and office. We will also confiscate his phone and computer. His attorneys are fighting the warrants, so it is taking longer than usual."

Guthrie said, "We are making good progress, but we need to keep at it. In particular, we still have no link between the attack on the Grahams and the shooting of Commissioner Peters. Keep after Cameron until those warrants are approved." He closed the meeting, and everyone went their separate ways.

CHAPTER 29:

DEVELOPER AND LAWYER MEETING - TOM MORRIS

James Cameron and Michael Bellows, his attorney, met the next day at Cameron's expensive office in WPB. Bellows was shown into the office by Cameron's good looking assistant. She wore a tight blue skirt and silk blouse open at the neck. She served them both coffee and Danish and then retired with both men watching her furtively. She smiled to think they were both so shallow.

Cameron put down his coffee and asked Bellows, "how did it go yesterday?" Bellows answered, "I have good news and bad news. The good news is that Pastor Morris knew about his Seminole Indian ancestor and his claim for property on Palm Beach Island. He gave me a full rundown on how he escaped as a slave in Georgia and worked his way through the swamps to the island that is now Palm Beach. He even told me the story of the land claim filed with the help of the Barefoot Mailman. He said he has the original deed that has been passed down through his family for generations." "That is wonderful news", said

Cameron. "I didn't think we would ever find a deed, since it is no longer recorded in Key West. What is the bad news?"

"The bad news is that Pastor Morris made it clear that he would never part with the deed, since it is a family heirloom. He is a person that is faithful to his church and his congregation. He will not be swayed by fancy cars or women. I don't know how you can get your hands on the deed, even if it is an original. "Let me worry about that problem", said Cameron. "Everyone has their price". Bellows replied, "Sometimes the price is not money or power. Anyway, I brought you a recording of the interview and a written transcription so you could study it further."

Cameron asked, "Is there" anyone else in Morris's family that might be interested in making a deal for the old land deed? It can't be worth much, except for sentimental value, since other people have owned the land for a long time". Bellows thought for a minute and looked at his notes on his tablet. "Pastor Morris has a son, Tom. Tom is not involved in the church, and he seems to have some minor scrapes with the law. He might be interested in making some fast money, even if it was against his father's wishes".

The two men moved on to discuss other cases and other issues before ending their meeting. "Let me know if you need anything else", Bellows said.

Cameron replied, "it's a shame to get this close and not be able to close the deal."

When Bellows was gone, Cameron called another number by heart. Again he heard a guttural voice, "What is it now?" "I have the plan to bring the hotel project into being, and to clean your funds in the process. All I need is the one job we discussed before. I even have a way to bring the pigeon to your dogs". They talked for a few more minutes, and Cameron ended the call with a smile on his face.

CHAPTER 30:
PASTOR MORRIS HIT BY TRAIN

Pastor Morris was tired. He had worked all day, and then had to go to a meeting at City Hall that night. The meeting was to discuss ways the City could help the Black community. As usual, the meeting was more about talking and less about action. Commissioner Nichols had called the meeting, and said they would look into helping the community, but Pastor Morris had heard it all before. He walked out to his old gray Toyota sedan, got in and started for his home near his church. It was a rainy night, and he put on the lights and windshield wipers. He drove down Lake Avenue, turned right on Federal, drove along the FEC railroad tracks as he went south, turned right again on 12th Ave. S. and stopped at the FEC railroad tracks because the big red lights on either side of the road were flashing. He saw the crossing gates, with red flashing lights, come down in front of his car. He wondered if this train was one of the old, slow freight trains, or one of those new high-speed trains.

He noticed a large black SUV pull behind him and stop.

He heard the whistle from the freight train approaching and thought he would have a long wait. Suddenly, the black SUV roared to life and surged forward to push the smaller Toyota. The SUV pushed the Toyota up the slope so that they broke the crossing gate. Pastor Morris held the brake down with all his strength, but the SUV was pushing his Toyota closer to the tracks. The toyota was making tire marks as they slid and the SUV tires were screaming as they spun while pushing the two vehicles closer to the tracks. Pastor Morris looked back and saw two heads in the windshield of the SUV. He then looked at the train as it roared closer to him. The SUV pushed the front of the Toyota onto the tracks. You could hear the tires of the SUV screeching, and his tires were slipping on the rain slicked pavement. He looked up and saw the train heading right at him. The light in the car was blinding and the sound was overwhelming. He thought, God help me. Somehow, he threw the car into drive, and floored the accelerator. Almost immediately, he felt a huge impact and heard the sound of metal screeching and tearing. He was thrown sideways like a ragdoll, and everything went black.

The train engineer was 48 and had been making this same freight run for many years. Tonight he was thinking about his vacation that was coming up with his wife and two high-school aged sons. They were going to the keys to fish and he could relax in the sun. He was watchful, because there had been several train accidents where people walked around closed train gates and were hit by trains. He did not want that to happen on his watch. His signal lights had all been green and he watched for the red lights to flash on rail crossings as he approached. Suddenly, he saw two vehicles break through the closed train gates and move toward the tracks. He cut power to the engine and through on the train brakes, but he knew it was hopeless. He had a heavy load of freight cars and it would take a half mile to stop them. He sounded the train horn and watched in horror as the engine plowed into the first small car. There was a huge crash and the car was thrown to the side like a toy. He looked back to see if the car burned, but it had been flipped over and spun completely around. He doubted if anyone could survive the crash, and knew he would have nightmares about it Eventually, the train came to a stop. He radioed his dispatcher that there had been a crash, to call 911 and to shut down both rail lines. He then climbed down from the engine to see if he could help the car's driver. He walked back along the tracks and saw the driver upside down in the car. He tried to open the door, but it was jammed shut. There was nothing he could do until the fire department arrived, so he walked back to federal highway to guide the first responders.

Detective Guthrie was eating a late supper with his wife and children. His cell phone rang, and his wife rolled her eyes. "Not again", she said. The kids looked away, as they had seen this happen too many times. Guthrie pulled the phone out and answered, "Detective Guthrie, what is it? An accident on the railroad line. Why is that mine?" The dispatcher said, "a witness saw a vehicle push another into the path of a train". "OK, I'll be there. I am sorry honey, but this sounds like an attempted murder. I don't know what is happening in Lake Worth Beach these days".

Guthrie rolled up on the crowded scene. There were sheriff deputies, fire trucks, and ambulances with flashing lights everywhere. He showed his badge to a patrolman, ducked under the tape, and spotted Sergeant Evans. "What happened Evans?" A man was hit by a northbound freight train. The train knocked the car 100 yards and destroyed it. The firemen are cutting the driver out of the car now with the jaws of life. Luckily, it was a freight train and not one of those high-speed trains. The 911 call from the scene said there was another vehicle involved, but it is not here now. There are signs that tires were smoking before the pastor's car was hit by the train". Guthrie replied, "Well, get all of these people back and shut off both sides of this crossing. Get CIS out here and impound the vehicle. Canvas the crowd to see if anyone took video. You can't do anything today without someone catching it. We 'll have to see if the victim makes it to learn what really happened. If he is still alive, I want a 24 hour guard on his hospital room".

Guthrie walked along the stopped freight train to the front of the big engine. He walked around the engine, and saw the mangled car about 100 yards back, where it had been thrown to the side. Firemen were still working to remove the victim. He noted that the most damage was to the left rear quarter of the car. If the engine had hit the left front quarter, they would be scraping up the body. He saw that a body was placed on a gurney, and then quickly moved to a waiting ambulance that roared off into the night. He then looked around for the train engineer. He saw him standing beside the big engine, smoking a cigarette. He walked over, flashed his badge and asked, "Are you the engineer?" The man nodded and shuffled his feet. He kept his head down and didn't raise his eyes. "What happened?" "I was coming north with 100 cars. I was within the speed and saw the gates drop at 12th Ave. S. Then I saw a big black SUV push the smaller car through the gate and onto the track. I could see the man in the car and thought for sure he was dead. Somehow, the train threw the car to the side instead of carrying it further down the tracks. By the time I got the engine stopped, the other SUV was long gone. I radioed dispatch and they called 911. I don't know what else I could have done". "I will want a statement later," said Guthrie, and walked back to his car. What was going on?

Dmitri called on his encrypted cell phone. "It went just as we planned. That Commissioner made sure the meeting ended at the right time. We picked up his car outside City Hall and trailed him to the railroad crossing. The crossing arms were just going down as he pulled onto 12th Ave. S. I pulled in behind him and waited until the freight train was close. We were able to push his little car with the SUV through the crossing arms and onto the track. At the last second, he tried to pull off the tracks, but the engine hit him and carried him down the tracks. I reversed, and the train barely missed us. I backed out onto Federal, and we got away clean". "Are you sure he is dead?" "He must be dead from the impact with that engine". "Well, confirm he is dead, or make sure he is dead by morning. Don't come back until you do".

CHAPTER 31:

SECOND ATTEMPT ON PASTOR MORRIS

As he left the scene, Detective Guthrie called Jack Price. "We may have had another attack". Jack was at Murray's, finishing up a steak and his second beer. He was stunned by the news. "What happened, he said a little breathlessly". "Not many details now, but someone pushed a car onto the FEC train tracks at 12th Ave. S. tonight. The car is mangled and they don't know if the victim will live or not. They were just putting him into the ambulance when I left. I don't know if it is going to the hospital or the morgue. As soon as I know, I will pass the word to you".

Jack finished his beer and paid for his meal. He wondered how this new attack could be related to the previous murders. Lake Worth Beach had never had a serial killer, and the media would go crazy, if there was another murder. He called Anna on her boat, and gave her the update. She had finished her dinner, washed the dishes, and was enjoying a second glass of wine in the cockpit. "Be ready to move quickly, once we get the call from Guthrie".

Thirty minutes later, he got the call from a tired Guthrie. "The victim was a black pastor. He is still alive, but has extensive injuries. They took him to John F Kennedy (JFK) hospital on Congress Ave. because it is the closest trauma center. I am sending a deputy to guard the victim, and you may want to send someone in case he wakes up. The media is going to be all over this attack of a black pastor, and we will get blamed for not protecting him. I already talked to the Sheriff and the Lake Worth Beach Mayor". "I will get right on it," said Jack. He ended the call, and immediately called Anna. "Please get over to JFK ASAP, and find Pastor Morris, the victim of the train crash. He is probably in surgery now in the trauma center. Guthrie is sending a guard, but you need to back him up, and try to get any word from the victim, if he wakes up". Anna said crossly, "I always wanted to spend the night in the trauma center, and hung up". Jack headed to the Sheriff substation to see if he could find any more information.

Anna dressed in black jeans, a pullover gray hoodie, and comfortable running shoes. She had been on many of these all-night assignments and wanted to be comfortable. Before she left, she unlocked her small metal gun case, and removed her Walther 9mm, short barrel pistol. She put it in a holster behind her back, under the hoodie. She added two extra magazines, locked the boat, and headed to the hospital.

JFK hospital was a large, multi-building complex, located in the City of Atlantis, on Congress Ave. between Lantana Road on the south and 6th Street S, on the north. JFK hospital was one of the largest hospitals in the county with 558 beds and was one of two hospitals with a trauma center. The hospitals included several towers with hospital beds, an emergency room, operating rooms, recovery room, cancer center, women's center, heart disease center as well as the typical supporting hospital departments. It included all major surgical specialties and was known for excellent care. The hospital was approximately three miles west of Lake worth Beach, and emergency cases were usually routed there.

At night, many of the normal entrances were closed, so Anna headed to the Emergency Room entrance. She parked and walked in the patient entrance. She saw a sheriff deputy, walked over and showed her identification. He told her the victim was a black male, named Pastor James Morris, and that he was in emergency surgery now. No one could get back there now. Anna nodded, and found a place to settle in. About an hour later, a female deputy escorted in a distraught black woman. Anna went over to comfort her, identified herself, and told her what had happened. She asked if Pastor Morris had any enemies. Mrs. Morris said, "No, he is well respected in the community. I can't understand how this could happen". Anna talked to the hospital staff and found out there was a surgery waiting room on the fourth floor near the operating rooms. She took Mrs. Morris to the waiting room, along with the deputy.

About midnight, a tired surgeon came out of surgery and approached Mrs. Morris. "Your husband was in a massive accident, and has many serious injuries, he said. We were able to stabilize him and stop most of the bleeding. The next 48 hours will be critical for him. He is in the recovery room now, and will be moved to intensive care (ICU) by morning". "Can I see him," said Mrs. Morris? "I'm afraid not yet. Maybe in the morning". Anna showed her credentials, and told the surgeon that Detective Guthrie had ordered round the clock protection for the victim. "You can't see him, but I will arrange for you to have a seat in the recovery room hallway. We can talk more, once he is in the ICU". Anna called the deputy, asked him to guard the entrance to the recovery room, and then went into the recovery room area with the surgeon.

The recovery room was large with room for 12 patients on hospital beds, six on each side. Each patient was connected to monitors at the head of their bed and surrounded by curtains to provide some privacy. There was a nurse's station for two nurses near the entrance. At this time of night, the recovery room was not very busy, and only one nurse and a few patients were there. She took a chair at the end of the room away from the patients. She then called Jack and updated him on the situation at the hospital. "I will come in the morning and relieve you at 7:00", said Jack. "Thanks for nothing," said Anna, "see you in the morning". She asked for a blanket and made herself as comfortable as possible,

Dmitri had burned the damaged black SUV, and changed to a modest white Ford Explorer, He learned that an ambulance took the driver of the car to a hospital. He guessed that the ambulance would go to JFK hospital, and went to the emergency room. He put a blue mask on his face before entering the Emergency Room, and told the receptionist that he had been sent by the city to check on Pastor Morris. The tired receptionist checked her computer and said, "he was brought in last night and is now in recovery. You will need to wait until morning to check with someone else". Dmitri thanked her, and went back outside to the car. "We have a big problem", he told Sergei. "That pastor is still alive. I don't know how that can be, but it is" Sergei cursed and muttered to himself. Dmitri said, "we have to find a way in, and end this guy".

Dmitri watched as cars pulled in and out of the parking lot. It was the night shift change. He saw both men and women coming out of the hospital, getting into their car and slowly driving away. "That is perfect", he said. They watched as a tall white man about 40 came out of the hospital, and drove away. They followed him out of the parking lot, and onto Congress Ave. He pulled into an all-night gas station at Lake Worth Ave. and Congress. As he got out of his car, Dmitri pulled up beside him, quickly got out and shot him in the head. He then pulled him into the back seat of the Explorer. He pulled the Explorer out of the gas station and tossed the man's car keys to Sergei, so he could follow in the other car. When they found a dark parking lot, they stopped and pulled the man out of the Explorer. Dmitri took the man's hospital identification, and his hospital scrubs. They fit him reasonably well. Dmitri then took the man's car and went back to JFK hospital, while Sergei got rid of the body and the Explorer. Dmitri did not like operations that went sideways like this, but he was going to finish this one.

When he got back to JFK hospital, he parked the car, and walked into the emergency room entrance. He followed the signs to the recovery room on the fourth floor near the operating rooms. He walked past the deputy into the recovery room and told the night nurse he had been called in to watch the critical patient in recovery. She was very busy and welcomed the help. Mr. Morris is in recovery 6 B located near the end of the room. I have checked on him twice and he seems to be doing well. I appreciate your help. Dmitri walked toward the bed located behind curtains in 6B. He pulled back the curtains and saw Morris covered in bandages and with multiple tubes providing oxygen, blood and medications. The monitor showed a steady pulse. It would be an easy job to use an extra pillow and smother him. He would then exit the back door before the night nurse could respond. He grabbed a pillow and moved toward the head of the victim.

Anna Henderson had been sitting in the chair at the end of the recovery room when she saw a man dressed in scrubs approach Pastor Morris's bed. Something did not seem right, so she stood up and walked to the curtained room. She entered through the curtains and saw the stranger with a pillow in his hand. She immediately yelled, "What are you doing?"

Dmitri pulled the silenced pistol from his back, but the scrubs slowed his draw. Anna was on him, before he could fire. She hit him hard and knocked him against the bed. He whipped the pistol up and hit her in the side of the head. She fell, but still screamed for help. He couldn't wait any longer without being trapped. He jumped over the fallen woman, pushed the curtains aside, and started to run for the back door. Just before he reached the door, he heard Anna yell "stop". He turned, brought up his pistol and they both fired at the same time. He felt a bullet slam through his side, and fired again at the woman lying on the ground. He then turned and ran through the back door. He frantically looked for an exit and saw a sign for stairs near him. He started down the stairs, holding his side, and feeling the blood ooze through his fingers. How had things gone this wrong? He had to get to the car and get away.

Anna heard both return shots and felt the bullet go through her left leg calf muscle. The other bullet twanged off the concrete floor near her head. She started to get up, but she was woozy from the shock of the bullet. Just then, the night nurse came in and saw her bleeding on the floor. She remembered the woman sent to protect Mr. Morris, and asked what happened. "The man in scrubs had a pillow and was going to smother your patient. I startled him and we struggled. He knocked me down and ran, but I got a shot off at him. He shot at me twice. I guess one of the bullets hit my leg. Quick, call 911 and get backup here in case he comes back." She still held her pistol, although her hands were now shaking.

The night nurse called 911, and then Anna asked her to call Jack Price. Anna took the phone and told a now wide-awake Jack about the intruder. "You need to get deputies to protect Mr. Morris and tape off the crime scene. I will be all right, but I can't go after him. I think I hit him, so there may be a blood trail". The night nurse bandaged her leg and wanted to give her a shot for the pain, but Anna would not let her until other officers arrived to protect them. She was placed on a bed, and soon everything went black.

Jack drove his BMW like a race car to the hospital. He pulled in with the tires smoking, jumped out and ran into the emergency room. There were a half dozen sheriff deputies there, and he was stopped before he could get to the recovery room. A full SWAT team rolled up and came into the emergency room. A call of shots fired at a major hospital had brought a full emergency response. Jack saw Detective Guthrie walk in, and Guthrie waved him over. "How is Anna", he asked. "She is in surgery for a bullet wound in her leg. It did not appear to be serious from what I heard. She saved Pastor Morris's life, and was in a shootout with the killer. We found a blood trail to the parking lot, but didn't catch him. He was a tall white male, and several people got a look at him. Hopefully, we can identify him this time. There is a full cordon around the hospital, and no one will get in or out without being thoroughly checked. We also have two officers sitting with Morris at the ICU". "When can I see Anna?" Jack asked. "It will be a couple of hours until she is out of recovery and into a private room. We will both go see her as soon as we can".

Dmitri had barely made it down to the first floor, and then out to the parking lot. Luckily, he wasn't stopped by anyone, although he heard sirens coming as he pulled out of the parking lot in the man's blue Prius. He knew he was losing a lot of blood, and made a rough bandage of his scrub top and pulled it to his side with his belt. He drove slowly, and fought to keep his eyes open. He called

Sergei, and asked him to meet him at the vacant parking lot where they had switched cars. Sergei reluctantly agreed, and said he would be there in 15 minutes. Dmitri pulled into a parking spot near the fence, and checked on his bandage. He knew he would need skilled help soon to survive. Finally, he saw Sergei drive into the parking lot. He still had the white Ford Explorer. He thought that was strange, since he had told Sergei to get rid of it, but he was in no position to complain now. Sergei got out of the Explorer, walked over to the driver side window and motioned him to lower the window. When he did, Sergei raised a pistol he had hidden by his side, and shot Dmitri twice in the forehead. Sergei grunted, "I am not going to clean up more of your messes". He then pulled the orderly's body from the back of the Explorer and dragged it to the passenger side of the Prius. He wedged it in the front seat and closed the door. He then brought out a gas can that he had purchased that night. He poured the gas into the driver side window, pulled out his lighter, and threw it into the Prius. Immediately, there was a whoosh as the gasoline caught fire and engulfed the Prius. Sergei turned, got back into the Explorer and drove away.

He called the special number, "Dmitri tried to finish the man from the railroad tracks while he was in the hospital. He failed again and didn't make it. I cleaned up his mess. Do you want me to finish the guy in the hospital?" "No, come back here. I have more important things for you to do".

CHAPTER 32:
ANOTHER MURDER

The day after the attack on Pastor Morris and Anna at JFK Hospital, Jack Price was sleeping in at his bungalow after the late night and gunshots in the hospital. About 10:00 am, the cell phone rang on his bedside table, and he reached for it. "Price here", he muttered. Detective Guthrie didn't sound much better than Jack. "I just got a call that patrolmen found a burned out car in a vacant lot at the Palm Beach State College campus on the corner of College and 6th Avenue South". "I am on my way". Jack got up, dressed and jumped in the BMW. He headed to Lucerne Avenue, turned west, went around the traffic circle at A Street, and got stopped by a train under the I-95 overpass. With traffic on Lake Worth Avenue, it took about 10 minutes to get to the college. He turned left at the light before Congress Avenue, and worked his way to a lot on the northeast side of the campus, near the canal. There were already several sheriff cruisers, ambulances, and a fire truck at the scene. He parked and got out several hundred feet from the scene. He walked over and found Guthrie. Guthrie updated him, "they found the car when students showed up for morning classes and called 911"

"There are two victims in the front seat, badly burned. The Coroner will have to identify the bodies and the cause of death, but it looks like it could be the work of our assassins. The car is registered to an orderly that works at JFK hospital. We have not been able to contact him this morning. I will ask the coroner to rush the autopsy since it may be tied to our case. We found two 9mm casings near the driver's side of the car. The killers are getting sloppy. I have deputies and CSI combing the area, but I don't expect much. This parking lot was deserted last night because it is mainly used during college baseball games. There are no CCTV cameras in the area.

Palm Beach State College is a large four-year state college that prepares students for careers in many fields, including police cadets, fire cadets, nursing and business. The college includes three campuses in the County. The Lake Worth Campus was the largest and it has many buildings, athletic fields, theater and fire tower. The parking lot was away from the main buildings, and was near a baseball field and a canal that separated the campus from the adjacent county park.

Detective Guthrie asked Jack how Anna was doing in the hospital. "I called her on my way here, and she seems much better. She said she wants to get out of the hospital today, but the doctor will have to see her before she can go. She was lucky in that shootout". As Jack said this, he could feel a lump form in his throat. He had not realized what Anna meant to him and how close he had come to losing her. I need to let her know how I feel, he thought.

Jack asked Guthrie, "Where does this leave us?" Guthrie scratched his head and said," At least, we now have one of the assassins to identify. We will follow him back to the rest of the killers. They made a big mistake last night, and Anna was there to stop them." She saved the pastor's life and fought off a trained assassin. You need to give her a raise." Jack nodded and kept quiet. He did not want to reveal what he felt for Anna.

CHAPTER 33:

JACK TALKS TO PASTOR MORRIS

Since Jack was near JFK Hospital, he decided to eat breakfast, and then visit Anna in the hospital. He stopped at the Dunkin Donuts shop on the Palm Beach State College Campus for a bacon, egg and cheese biscuit, and a large coffee. After downing that quick breakfast, he promised himself to have a better lunch, and headed south on Congress to the hospital. He rode up the elevator, and found Anna watching television and waiting impatiently for her doctor. She said, "I am getting out of this hospital today". Jack smiled at her and said, "You scared me last night, and I don't ever want to lose you. I…I need you too much as a partner. Anna smiled at Jack, but her eyes were sad. /She said, "I was wondering if you would ever say something partner". Jack leaned over and kissed her tenderly on the forehead. That wasn't what Anna had been hoping.

After the tender moment had passed, Anna said, "How can I help you catch this guy?"

"Can you tell me more about the shooting last night?" "I was at the end of the recovery room sitting in a chair, when I saw this tall guy in scrubs walk into Pastor Morris' room. I got up, walked over and pulled the curtain aside to see this guy with a pillow starting to smother Morris. I didn't think, and just yelled at the guy and tackled him. He turned and knocked me down, and then ran. I managed to pull my pistol and yelled for him to stop. He turned and brought his pistol up, so I fired once from the floor. I think I hit him. He fired twice at me before running out the door. One of the bullets hit my leg. The nurse came in and I called you for help. I don't remember much after that". Jack said, "you saved Pastor Morris and definitely hit the killer. There was a blood trail down the stairs and out to the parking lot. By the time I got down there, he was gone. They found the guy this morning, burnt to a crisp in a car, with two bullets in his head. There was also a second body that hasn't been identified yet. Whoever is behind these murders is ruthless with his own people, as well as anyone that gets in the way," Anna shuddered slightly and said, "I guess I was lucky last night. I just reacted to protect Pastor Morris." "Jack said, you did great and took out one of the two professional assassins that have been terrorizing this town. I am very proud to call you partner," Anna was surprised and pleased by Jack's statement about being a partner, but she was also looking for a different kind of partnership. "Thanks Jack, I appreciate that." We can talk more after we take down the other killer."

They talked a while longer and then Jack said he was going to check on Pastor Morris. He went up to the sixth floor to the ICU ward. He showed his credentials to the nurse station and also to the two deputies at the entrance to the ICU. The nurse said that Pastor Morris had recently awakened, but was in considerable pain. "Can I talk to him", asked Jack. "Yes, but don't stress him or tire him out", said the nurse.

When Jack walked into Pastor Morris' ICU station, Morris was half awake. "Pastor Morris, I am a detective working with the Sheriff to find your attacker", he said. "Can you tell me what happened?" "I was on my way home from a special meeting at City Hall called by Commissioner Nichols. I try not to go out at night. After the meeting, I got in my car and drove towards home down Federal. Just as I turned onto 12th Ave. S, the railroad lights flashed and I stopped before the gates came down. I could see the train coming. Then a big SUV hit me from behind and started pushing me through the railroad gates onto the track. I held the brakes as hard as I could, but my car is much lighter than that big SUV. I looked back and saw two men in the SUV. I heard their tires screeching, and saw that I was on the center of the track with the train coming right at me. Suddenly, it was like the Lord said, "Gun it." I gunned the engine forward just at the last second, and moved just enough so the train hit the rear of my car. I blacked out then and didn't wake up until a few minutes ago". The pastor's pulse was going up as he recounted the story, and the nurse told Jack to stop. "Thanks Pastor, I am so glad that you made it. Get better soon".

Jack walked back out of the hospital and thought, that SUV and two men sounds just like the two assassins from the other two murders. How could Pastor Morris have anything that would make him a target? What could the three attacks have in common?

CHAPTER 34:

COMMISSIONER NICHOLS INTERVIEWS

As Price drove back from the hospital, he called Detective Guthrie and updated him on Pastor Morris. Detective Guthrie said, "what are the odds that Pastor Morris would come to those railroad tracks at the same time as the train was crossing?" "Morris said that Commissioner Nichols had called a special meeting. I wonder if Commissioner Nichols also ended the meeting at a special time so that Morris would be driving home as the train gates came down". "That would take some pretty close timing". Guthrie looked for his notes on Commissioner Nichols. "We checked Nichols incoming and outgoing phone calls and meeting calendar. He had several phone calls from Cameron during the last thirty days. The last call was two days before the special meeting with Pastor Morris. He also had a lunch meeting with Cameron just before Commissioner Peters was killed." Jack said "all of that is circumstantial evidence. We don't have enough to charge him" Guthrie said, "No, but we can sweat him. If that doesn't work, we can get a search warrant. Come over to the substation after lunch. I will make an appointment to see Commissioner Nichols in the City Hall office. You can come along."

Jack called Anna to see how she was doing. She was at home in her Catalina sailboat, keeping her leg elevated. "It's tough to get up and down the ladder into the main cabin with a gimpy leg", she said. "How about lunch," Jack asked. "That sounds great." "I will pick you up." Jack went east on 6th Ave. S to Federal and then turned south to the marina. He pulled into the parking lot, walked to Anna's boat, and called, "permission to come aboard." She stuck her head out of the main cabin and said, "give me a few minutes." She appeared in the cockpit of the Catalina, and Jack helped her down to the dock. She wore tan slacks, a blue silk shirt, and boat shoes. She had a slight limp as they walked slowly off the dock to the BMW. "What about Murray's for lunch", asked Jack? "That sounds fine". "We have an appointment with Guthrie after lunch, and I thought you deserve to be there. I can brief you during lunch".

When they reached Murray's, Jack let Anna out on the sidewalk so she could get an outside table. He went to park in a lot on a side street and she took a seat at one of the open tables. A waiter came and she ordered red wine for herself and a beer for Jack. When Jack arrived, they toasted their new partnership, and Jack described his last call with

Guthrie. Anna said, "I always thought Nichols was slimy, but I didn't think he would go this far." Jack said, "We can't prove anything yet, but it will be interesting to see what Nichols says this afternoon." Anna ordered a chicken wrap and Jack ordered a Philly cheese steak. They made small talk until the meals came and then ate while they enjoyed the sunshine.

After lunch, Jack drove to the Sheriff substation, showed his identification to the receptionist, and then went up in the elevator with Anna. Detective Guthrie was surprised to see Anna but didn't say anything. Jack asked Guthrie, "How do you want to play the meeting with Commissioner Nichols?" "I think we act like we have all the evidence we need to put Nichols away as an accomplice to the murders. He is a weak link and won't like the sound of serious jail time. If he makes a deal, we can work with the District Attorney to reduce his sentence". Jack said, "that should ruin his day. We need to monitor his phone calls and outside meetings to see if he leads us back to someone else." Guthrie called the Sheriff's technical section and made sure they were monitoring Nichol's calls.

Detective Guthrie and Jack walked the two blocks from the Sheriff substation to City Hall, while Anna drove Jack's car to the parking lot. They walked up the front steps of City Hall and the stairs to the second floor. Anna took the small elevator to the second floor and met them in the hallway. They asked the receptionist to tell Commissioner Nichols they were there. In about five minutes, Commissioner Nichols came out and escorted them to the City Manager's office, where there was a conference table. The City manager was gone, so they could use the room. Commissioner Nichols started by asking Detective Guthrie, "What is this all about? I thought you were the only one coming." Detective Guthrie said, "Mr. Price and Miss Henderson are part of the Task force investigating the two murders, and the attack on Pastor Morris. We are hoping that you can help us with the timeline of your meeting with Pastor Morris yesterday."

Commissioner Nichols stated, "Pastor Morris attended a special meeting to discuss the needs of the black churches in District 1 on the Southwest side of Lake Worth Beach. I try to maintain communications with the black pastors to better understand the people in that area." "And when did you call that special meeting?" "I was in a hurry and called the meeting three days ago. I am a busy man." "And how many pastors were at this meeting?" "Pastor Morris and the two pastors from the other two churches on 15th Avenue S. They are very knowledgeable and could provide the information I requested."

Jack continued, "We are part of the task force investigating three murders here in Lake Worth

Beach. That total would have been four, except that two attempts on Pastor Morris's life were foiled last night. I am the liaison with the FBI, and have been investigating ties that the developer, James Cameron, has with organized crime. We know that you have been in contact with Cameron, and that Cameron was against the election of Peters. Did Cameron ask you to set up the special meeting and end the meeting at the right time to lure Pastor Morris to the railroad, just when a train was coming? Your involvement with Cameron could lead to charges as an accessory to murder and attempted murder, as well as charges of racketeering. How would the news media handle that?"

Nichols' eyes were big and round, and he was sweating profusely, even though the room was cool. "You can't do that", he screamed. "I don't know anything about these murders". Guthrie said, "We know you are involved, and it is only a matter of time before we learn the whole story. If you want to stay off murderers' row, you need to tell us everything you know and make a deal with the District Attorney to reduce your sentence". Nichols looked like he might be sick. Anna chimed in, "I was there last night when the assassin tried again to murder Pastor Morris. I shot one of them and he is singing like a bird. If he makes a deal before you do, you will be out of luck."

Commissioner Nichols looked from one of the three investigators to the other like a cornered rabbit. He couldn't imagine being locked behind bars. "Look, I didn't know anything about those murders. I may have had some phone conversations and meetings with James Cameron, but I am not involved in any of these crimes. If you want to talk with me further, set up a meeting with my attorney. This meeting is over."

As they left City Hall, Jack said, "We rattled Nichols today." Let's see who he calls. He is the weak link in these murders." Guthrie added, "We are monitoring his calls, and I will have a team follow him if he goes out. I will call his attorney for another meeting to keep the pressure on."

Nichols called Cameron on his cell phone. "We need to meet. The Sheriff Detective and two private eyes were just in my office. They are accusing me of being involved in the murders with you. You need to keep me out of this mess." Cameron growled, "You knew what you were doing when you took my money. They can't prove anything. If they could, they would have arrested you. Keep your mouth shut and this will blow over. There is a lot more money coming if this project is successful." Nichols fumed about Cameron's response, but he knew he couldn't walk away from Cameron after taking so much money. He left City Hall for a drink.

Two days later, Detective Guthrie, Sergeant Evans, Jack and Anna met with Commissioner Nichols and his attorney. Detective Guthrie had insisted that the meeting be held in the Sheriff Substation second floor conference room. He wanted home field advantage and to make Nichols sweat. When Nichols and the attorney walked in, Guthrie asked if they wanted coffees and Nichols replied, "No, let's get this meeting over."

Detective Guthrie started the meeting by saying the interview would be recorded and introducing each person for the record. He then said, "we are part of the task force investigating the murders of Commissioner Peters, two people on the Graham's yacht and the attempted murder of Pastor James Morris. These are very serious crimes. We have reason to believe that Mr. Cameron is involved in these crimes, and that you have cooperated with Mr. Cameron in these illegal activities. We know that you are involved. If you cooperate with us by telling us everything you know, we will ask for leniency for you from the District Attorney."

Commissioner Nichols stated, "I told you that I am not involved in any of these crimes, and I resent you continuing to harass me. I will be contacting the County Sheriff to have you taken off this case." Guthrie said, "Mr. Nichols, we have subpoenaed your phone and email records. We also have recordings of recent phone calls that you made to Mr. Cameron." He handed Commissioner Nichols a transcript of his call to Cameron after the last meeting. This phone call is proof that you have accepted bribes from Mr. Camaeron and that you are involved in the murders. You are facing serious jail time. This is your last chance to come clean and tell us what you know."

Commissioner Nichols was sweating and loosened his tie. He turned and conferred with his attorney for a few minutes. His face turned white, and he shook his head. He then turned back to Guthrie and said, "I didn't know he was doing anything like this. He wanted to buy the old pool site on the beach and redevelop it into a hotel and casino. He wanted me to get three votes for the purchase, but I told him Commissioner Peters would oppose it. Then, he asked me to have a special meeting with Pastor Morris and end it at 9:05 pm. I thought that was a strange request but told him I would do it." Detective Guthrie chimed in, "you have just admitted to being an accessory to attempted murder. Why were you so willing to help Cameron?" Nichols looked thoroughly defeated. "If I help you, can you get me off?" Detective Guthrie said, "we will tell the District Attorney that you cooperated, and ask for leniency, but you are through as a commissioner and are looking at serious jail time. You have the right to an attorney…." Commissioner Nichols told them about several large and illegal donations from Cameron, as well as offers of much more when the pool deal was completed. He also confirmed that

Cameron had asked him to get three votes for the pool deal, in violation of the Florida Sunshine Act.

When they were done questioning Nichols, Sergeant Evans led him out of the conference room in cuffs. Detective Guthrie, Jack and Anna looked at each other and at their notes. "This case has broken wide open", said Jack.

CHAPTER 35:

FIFTH TASK FORCE MEETING

The Task Force members trooped into the City Hall Conference Room the next morning at 9:00 am. Detective Guthrie had called the meeting because of several breaks in the case. Everyone had an expectant air as they waited for Guthrie to begin the meeting. The large white board had fewer names and photographs, which indicated that the case was progressing.

Guthrie welcomed everyone and called for order right at 9:00 am. "Folks, you have all been working hard, and we are finally getting some breaks in the case. But we are not done yet, and I need you to redouble your efforts until we find all of the killers". Everyone in the room sat up straighter, as they caught Guthrie's implication. "Two nights ago there were two attempts to kill Pastor James Morris. Both were unsuccessful, due to a combination of God's grace and the skill of Anna Henderson". Anna blushed at the complement. "The killer was wounded, but got away from JFK Hospital. Yesterday, we found another murder scene with a burned car and two men inside. The coroner has now confirmed the two men as an orderly that was working at JFK Hospital, and a tall man with three bullet wounds. The first bullet wound was in his side, fired by Miss Henderson, and the other two were point blank shots in his head, fired by another assassin. The orderly was killed by the same gun that killed the waiter at the Graham home, and Commissioner Peters. That gun was recovered in the burned car. The two shots by the unknown assassin are from a different 9 mm pistol. Obviously, the tall man in the car that was shot three times was the first professional assassin. The coroner has not identified him, but we are sending DNA and dental records to the FBI and Interpol for help in the identification. The killers are the two assassins seen at both the Graham home and the Peters shooting. But we still don't know their motive or who hired them. We need to identify the first man, so we can find his associates and nail them".

"The second break in the case came yesterday, when we interviewed Commissioner Nichols. He claims he knew nothing about any murder plots, and implicated a big-league developer, James Cameron. He said Cameron talked about Peters being an impediment to his plans to buy the Lake Worth pool site. Nichols also said Cameron asked for the special meeting with Pastor Morris, and specified the time it should end, so that Morris would be caught at the FEC railroad tracks going home".

"I still don't have any connection between the attack on Graham, the attack on Peters and the attack on Morris. We have checked Graham's case files, and don't see any connection to Cameron's developments. Morris generally supported environmental and public causes, but had not taken a position on the pool, because his parishioners don't use it."

"We need to check every scrap of evidence and witnesses to find out anything you can about Nichols, Cameron and Graham. Recheck all of the phone records, emails and meeting calendars to see if there are connections. We have a warrant to search Mr. Cameron's house, phone and business for connections to the murders. I want this case wrapped up before there are other murders".

After the meeting, Jack and Anna talked in the conference room, before they left. Jack asked Anna to help search the Cameron properties with other sheriff deputies, and investigate any leads between Cameron and the murders. He said he would check back with the FBI and Interpol to see if there was any new information from Europe.

CHAPTER 36:

CAMERON HOUSE SEARCH

The next day, the Sheriff SWAT team, Sergeant Evans, several deputies and Anna Henderson executed the search warrant at the Cameron's expansive mansion in Manalapan, an exclusive beach community south of Palm Beach. Manalapan stretched from the ocean to the intracoastal water way, and included an island in the intracoastal waterway. It stretched from Lantana Blvd in the North to the Boynton Beach inlet in the South.

Cameron's mansion covered two acres from A1A roadway to the intracoastal waterway. It was four stories high, so that you could see the Atlantic Ocean from its upper levels. It also had a tunnel under A1A, with a beach house so that you could get to the beach. The view from the road was restricted by a high wall and iron gates. The mansion was set back from the road, and was a Mediterranean design, with arched entrance doors, towers on both ends and two stories showing from the Atlantic ocean side. The Intracoastal side of the mansion was four stories built of stone, with balconies, swimming pool, guest quarters and garages. The mansion itself was 20,000 square feet, with 15 bedrooms and 20 baths. No expense had been spared after Cameron had purchased and then renovated the mansion.

Sergeant Evans knocked, showed the house manager the warrant, and waved the deputies inside. The house manager said that Mr. Cameron was not at the house. He called him and left a message that the house was being searched. The SWAT team stayed inside their vehicle, and seemed disappointed that there was no resistance. The deputies fanned out through the house, looking for computers, phones, hidden safes, and offices. They brought out boxes of evidence to be inspected by the task force. Anna and Evans walked through the mansion, and directed the search. They were amazed at the size and beauty of the home. Evans said, "no wonder real estate costs so much". Anna smiled and replied, "he didn't pay for all of this with legal money. We just have to find the connections". Anna noticed the calendar on Cameron's desk. It held a listing of meetings that Cameron attended or had planned. Most were business meetings, but one held her interest. "Cameron met someone at the Palm Beach County Historical Society. I wonder what that was about". When the search was complete, Anna found the number for the Historical Society on Google. She called and set up a meeting with the Historian for the next day.

A similar warrant was being executed at Mr. Cameron's business office on the 18th floor of a downtown WPB skyscraper. Again, Cameron was not available, and the search team brought out many boxes of material from his office. The task force team was going to have a lot of work.

CHAPTER 37:
ANNA AND THE HISTORIAN

The next morning at 10:00 am, Anna walked up the steps of the Old Court House, which was located just west of the County Administration building. She opened the big oak doors and went to the receptionist. She showed her identification and said, "I am following up on a meeting requested last month by Mr. James Cameron". The receptionist looked at their computer calendar, and said, "Mr. Cameron met with Mr. Phillip Summers, the County historian. He is retired, and still comes in three days per week. You are lucky that he is here". Anna asked if she could see him.

The historian came out to meet her in about five minutes. "Hello, I am Anna Henderson", she said and showed her identification. "I am Phillip Summers", he said. "What can I do to help you?" "I understand that you had a meeting with Mr. James Cameron a few weeks ago. Do you remember what you discussed?" "It was a strange meeting, but I have many of those. He had an interest in land owned or claimed by the Seminole Indians. I described the history of the early Seminole Indians in this area. Most of them lived in swampy areas in the interior of the state. He asked for copies of maps showing these early lands. He then asked if any of the Seminole land holdings were on or near the ocean. I told him I would look into it. Over the next few days, I was able to investigate two early claims. One man lived on what is now Palm Beach. He was a runaway slave, named Aloyisus James, and he made a land claim with the help of "the Barefoot Mailman." The other was the site of the second Seminole Indian war, which is now a State Park in Jupiter". Anna asked if she could have copies of the documents sent to Mr. Cameron. Mr. Summers promised to have them copied and sent to her office. Anna thanked him and hurried out of the Old Court House.

She called Jack Price to give him an update. "It appears that Mr. Cameron was investigating land that was originally owned by Seminole Indians", she told him. "I don't know how that ties to any of the murders". Jack thought and said, "don't the Seminoles own all of the casinos in Florida? If Cameron could get his hands on land owned by the Seminole Indians, he might be able to sell it to the present-day Seminole Indians for use as a new casino site. We know he was trying to redevelop the Lake Worth Beach pool site. What if that is the location of the old Seminole Indian land? It would be worth millions as a casino site". "But why would they try to kill Pastor Morris?' "From my short interview with him, he seems to be a Pastor concerned for the welfare of his people, and not looking for wealth. Maybe Cameron decided it would be easier to get control of the land if the Pastor was out of the picture. We need to find out if there is any connection between the Seminole Indians and Pastor Morris. We also need to investigate all of Pastor Morris's relatives to see if any were connected with Cameron". Anna said, "I am on it".

That afternoon, Anna went to see Pastor Morris in the hospital. He was out of ICU and had his own room in a different part of JFK hospital. After checking in with the receptionist, Anna went to his room and knocked before entering. There was still a deputy sitting outside Pastor Morris's door. She heard a weak voice telling her to enter. "Hello, I am Anna Henderson, a private detective working with the Sheriff's department. I would like to ask you some additional questions."

CHAPTER 38:

CLOSING IN ON CAMERON

The next day, Jack arrived at the City Hall for another task force meeting feeling excited and upbeat. Things were finally going their way, and he thought the case was nearly solved. He walked up the stairs to the second floor conference room and took his accustomed place. Detective Guthrie came in and opened the meeting. There were noticeably fewer agents at the table, because several had been reassigned to other cases. The case would go cold if they couldn't solve it soon. "Good morning everyone. We have several new developments today, and we are narrowing the field of suspects". "Jack, why don't you update us?"

"We have had three major developments in the last two days. First, Commissioner Nichols has admitted that he was involved in a scheme to sell the Lake Worth Beach pool site to Mr. James Cameron, a major developer, who was paying Nichols through large illegal donations. He also admitted setting up Pastor Morris by calling a special meeting with Morris, and then ending the meeting at a specific time that placed Morris at the FEC tracks as a train approached. Commissioner Nichols maintains that he did not know of any murder plots, but he is being held pending further investigation".

"Second, we obtained a warrant and searched Mr. James Cameron's house and business. Mr. Cameron was not at either location, and has not come forward to answer questions. We are still sifting through evidence, but it is clear from phone records and calendar notices that Cameron and Nichols were in close contact. Cameron recently tried to obtain Commission approval to buy the Lake Worth Beach pool site on the beach, so that he could redevelop it. He knew that Commissioner Peters would oppose him, and that is a clear motive Cameron had for killing Peters. So far, we don't have any direct ties between Mr.Graham and Cameron, but we are investigating the possibility that they had business dealings".

"Third, just yesterday we talked to the Palm Beach County historian, and found out that Mr. Cameron was searching for properties previously owned or claimed by Seminole Indians. The historian identified two sites in Palm Beach County, one of which was the Lake Worth Beach Casino and pool site. We have just learned that Pastor James Morris is the legal heir of the Seminole Indian that claimed the land, and that he holds the actual land claim, which has been passed down through the generations. Pastor Morris had made it clear he would not part with the land claim. This gave Cameron a clear motive for killing Pastor Morris".

Sergeant Evans described the searches of Mr. Cameron's house and business. "We conducted simultaneous searches of Mr. Cameron's mansion on Manalapan and his business offices in West Palm Beach. Approximately ten deputies and several CSI personnel were involved in each of the searches. Mr. Cameron was not at either site, and there was no resistance once we presented the proper warrants. We found and confiscated phones and computers at both sites. We also found and opened safes at both locations that contained substantial amounts of cash and gems. We searched for phone and business records to determine any third parties involved with Mr. Cameron in the Lake Worth Beach casino project. We also confiscated a large number of files from both sites. We will be assigning these files to each of you for further investigation.

Detective Guthrie took over. "We need to find James Cameron, and determine his movements over the last few weeks. We also need to trace several calls made to and from Cameron. The phone calls were to untraceable encrypted phones, but we have now asked the NSA to assist in tracking these phone calls. We have issued a warrant to arrest Mr. Cameron on suspicion of murder and have put out an All-Points Bulletin (APB) to arrest Mr.

162

Cameron. If you have any further information on Cameron or his associates, please provide it ASAP."

After the meeting broke up, Jack walked over to Detective Guthrie. "We are closing in now. I can feel i.". Guthrie muttered, "Yes, but we can't let this guy get away."

Several miles from Lake Worth City Hall, Sergei received a phone call on his encrypted phone at about the same time. "Cameron has been compromised, and is too hot for us to continue the project". Sergei asked, "what do you want me to do?" "We need to clean up loose ends, so nothing comes back to us. You already took care of Dmitri. He was sloppy. Cameron is the only person that knows the connection with us. I know he is planning to leave the country tonight. Be at the Boca Raton airport, and don't miss". "I understand, boss".

That afternoon, Jack received a phone call from Detective Guthrie. "We got a tip from the fixed base operator (FBO), Boca Air, at the Boca Raton airport. They received a request from Cameron's pilot to fuel and provision his Citation for a trip to Dallas. They had seen the APB, and let us know. The flight is scheduled for 7:00 pm. Do you want in on the takedown?" Jack said, "you bet". "We will be meeting at the adjacent Easy Air FBO at 5:00 pm. Please coordinate with the FBI and airport security, so that they know we are coming. We can't let him get in the airplane. We will wait until his luggage has been taken out to the plane, and he is on foot to surround the plane and stop him. We already have enough to charge and hold him on lesser crimes while we gather more evidence of the murders".

Jack met Anna at Murray's for a drink, and brought her up to speed. "Please watch the Graham's and make sure they don't also run. We don't know if there is a connection between Graham and Cameron or not". After his drink, Jack drove the BMW down Federal Highway, turned west onto 6th Avenue S. and then south on I-95 at the interchange. It was beginning the afternoon rush hour, so the five lanes on South I-95 were full, and traffic was building. Luckily, there were no accidents, so he made good time to Yamato Road in Boca Raton. Following his GPS, he drove east on Yamato, south on NW 40th Street, and finally south on Airport Road to the fixed base operator. Airport Road ran parallel between I-95 on the west and the airport runway on the east.

Jack parked at Easy Air FBO, walked through the lobby and into the large hanger. A crowd of detectives, SWAT team, FBI and deputies were milling around. In addition, two sheriff vehicles, a SWAT truck and four black Expeditions were lined up, facing the open hanger doors toward the runway. Jack walked over to Detective Guthrie. Guthrie said, "We have a spotter on the roof with a

164

radio. When they see Cameron walk out of Boca Air, the Boca Air manager will lock the door, and we will surround him and block the plane. We don't want him taking any hostages inside the FBO". Everyone checked their equipment and tried to keep their excitement in control.

At 6:00 pm, a black Mercedes arrived at Boca Air. The FBO manager called Guthrie and alerted him. "Everybody mount up. It looks like he is trying to get away early". Jack caught a ride in the back seat of Guthrie's expedition. He was carrying a 40 caliber Smith & Wesson pistol in a shoulder holster, but thought there was too much firepower already. The luggage was brought out and loaded in the plane. Then at 6:15 pm, the spotter radioed that a man in a suit coat and a younger woman walked out the door of the FBO and to the plane. Guthrie yelled, "Go, Go, Go". Immediately, the procession of vehicles roared out of the hanger and across the 200 yards of tarmac to the waiting jet. Cameron saw them coming and started to run to the plane, but quickly was cut off. Men jumped out of their vehicles and yelled for everyone to stop and raise their hands. Looking at the number of guns, there was no doubt that Cameron was caught. Guthrie and Jack jumped out of the Expedition, and started toward Cameron to make the arrest. Just as they got within 50 feet of the suspects, a sharp crack of a high-powered rifle was heard, and Cameron crumpled to the pavement. Everyone else ducked down on instinct. Several people yelled, "shots fired". The SWAT team swung their rifles in all directions, trying to protect the officers and find the sniper. Jack looked to the northwest in the direction where the shot was fired. There was a white van pulling off the Yamato Road overpass. He thought he saw a sign on the side of the van, but he could not see details. He thought it could be the assassin. He called out to Guthrie and asked him to have the spotter on the roof look for the white van. Guthrie immediately radioed the spotter. A few seconds later, the spotter called back and confirmed that a white van was going east from the airport on Yamato Road. He could not see any signage on the van but reported that it had ladders on a ladder rack on top of the van.

The scene was bedlam for a few moments, and then training took over. Guthrie and Jack rushed to Cameron, while other detectives grabbed the young woman. Guthrie was hoping for Cameron to talk, but he quickly saw the bullet had gone through the side of his head. They called for the scene to be locked down as a crime scene, and called the coroner, although it was already obvious the time and cause of death. Jack asked Guthrie to put out an APB on the white van, but Guthrie just groaned and said, "that would cover at least 10,000 vans in Boca Raton". Neither Guthrie or Jack could believe what had happened. "How did they know?" asked Jack. "Why would they kill Cameron, if he was the mastermind?" Guthrie growled, "evidently, there is still an assassin out there".

Two miles away, the white van pulled into a rented warehouse. Sergei and another Spetnaz bodyguard got out and closed the overhead door. Sergei pulled out an encrypted cell phone, called a number and said, "It is done." The guttural voice said, "Good, make sure you are not followed and get back here." Sergei ended the call, walked to a nondescript Chevy Blazer and left the van in the warehouse. He would make at least three circles through Boca Raton and Delray to assure he wasn't followed before heading back. It had been a good morning.

CHAPTER 39:

AFTERMATH

The next day, Jack and Anna walked up the steps of City Hall to the conference room for another called task force meeting. The Sheriff was there again, and had called a press release for after the meeting. The Sheriff started the meeting by thanking everyone involved, particularly Detective Guthrie, for solving the serial murder. He said, "both the assassin that killed our citizens and James Cameron, the mastermind of this plot, have both been killed. In addition, Commissioner Nichols has been arrested and charged with conspiracy to commit murder. We know that there is another hired assassin that probably killed both the first assassin and Mr. Cameron. We have asked the FBI to continue that investigation, since the assassin is undoubtedly out of the state, and probably out of the country. Detective Guthrie and the Lake Worth Beach substation will continue to close the case, and the task force members are released to their normal duties".

After the meeting, Jack walked over to Detective Guthrie. "That is one way to close a case", he said. Guthrie growled, "you heard the man. He closed the case and declared that justice was done". Jack replied, "but there is still another assassin out there. And whoever heard of the mastermind being killed by his own assassin. There must be someone else calling the shots that we haven't discovered". Guthrie just said, "Let's just move on and call this a win. I have five other cases that need to be solved". Jack couldn't let it go. "Look, someone ordered a hit on Mr. Graham and his wife. Someone ordered the hit on Cameron, right under our noses. I will not stop until we find them". Detective Guthrie sighed and said "Good Luck". He turned and walked out of City Hall. Jack looked at Anna and said, "it looks like we are on our own. Let's get out of here". They walked out of City Hall and two blocks down the street to Murray's for a needed drink.

Jack ordered a beer for himself and a glass of wine for Anna. When the drinks came, Jack said, "can you believe that the Sheriff just quit on this case?" Anna took a long sip of her wine and replied, "that is the difference between police work and politics. All the politicians want is a win that they can talk about in front of the media. It is why most detectives keep a box of old case files that were never solved. We can't let them go". Jack said, "Well, I am not going to let a murderer go free because it is hard to find them. Will you help me?" Anna said, "Of course I will help. I can still feel the bullet that went through my leg. I won't let the

169

person responsible go free." They finished their drinks and went back to Jack's office.

CHAPTER 40:
NEW INFORMATION

Jack and Anna spent the next two days going back over the case to find any new information that might lead to the killer. Anna went back over the Graham files and noticed the reference to the Ukrainian General. "We never did get information from Interpol about this guy". Jack went back to find anything more about the first assassin. "We never got an identification for this guy. If we knew his identity, he might lead us to the other assassin".

Jack called the coroner's office to see if they had any leads from the assassin's DNA. "We just got a DNA match through Interpol. The man's name was Dmitri Filepov. He was a Spetnatz captain in the Russian FSB until five years ago. Since then, he does not show up on any records in Europe or the US". Jack muttered, "that sounds like an assassin to me". He called his contact at Interpol. "We have identified one of the assassins in the quadruple murder case", he said. "The man's name is Dmitri Filepov, and he is ex-Spetsnaz. Do you have any record of known associates while he was in Spetsnaz, or later. We think he may be part of a ring of hired assassins". The Interpol agent promised to check and get back with them.

Jack also asked his Interpol contact to check again on the Ukrainian General related to Mrs. Graham. "We need to follow that lead to determine if it is a real threat or not. They could still be out there trying to kill this couple".

CHAPTER 41:

JACK'S PHONE CALL
WITH INTERPOL.

The night after the final Press Release from the Sheriff about the case, Jack received a phone call about 11:30 pm. He was halfway in the bottle at his bungalow. "Sorry to call you so late, I know there is a seven hour time difference between you and here in Poland". "That's okay, I haven't thought of anything except the case for days", Jack said, being careful not to slur his words. "What do you have?" "We have been following up on the rumors about Mrs. Graham's relative in the Ukrainian army. We were able to contact him by phone and then interview him in Ukraine today. Obviously, I can't tell you where the interview took place. It turns out that this Ukrainian General has now been placed in charge of all land armies within Ukraine for the war against Russia. He is in constant contact with President Zelensky and all of the Ukrainian forces fighting in different areas. Obviously, he is a prime target of the Russian military, and his whereabouts are closely guarded. He confirmed that he receives daily death threats and has had his headquarters bombed repeatedly. He also has been threatened with the death of all his family and relatives, unless Ukraine quickly gives up. He has taken steps to have his relatives in Ukraine and the rest of Europe hidden and protected. But he did not know Mrs. Graham was in the United States. He cautioned that Russia has used hired assassins in the past and asked that Mrs. Graham and her family receive immediate protection from the US. He will be formally sending this request through President Zelensky to the White House".

Jack rocked back in his chair, "maybe we really do have Russian assassins here in Lake Worth Beach". "What do you mean?" "There was already an attempt on Mrs. Graham's life, and now five other people have been killed. Witnesses reportedly saw two tall men dressed in black at both of the first two crime scenes. All of the attacks were professional hits. We have identified one of the dead men as a previous Spetnatz agent named Dimitri Filipov. Were you able to find any connections with other Spetsnaz agents?" "Yes, Dmitri Filipov was in a special operations unit with another agent, Sergei Yuryeva, until about five years ago. They both left Spetsnaz and became bodyguards for a Russian Oligarch, with strong ties to Putin". "What is the Oligarch's name and where is he located?" "His name is Victor Sidorov. He could be anywhere. He has mansions in Moscow, Crimea, Paris, Monte Carlo and even Palm Beach". Jack sucked in his breath. "You mean this billionaire and his two goons could be here?" "He keeps a 737 aircraft and pilots ready so he can go wherever he wants". Jack shouted, "We're 60 miles from Miami, and have several Russian billionaires in Palm Beach. You better talk to your CIA contact and get major help before this situation blows up further. Thanks for the information. I know I won't sleep tonight".

Jack hung up and called Anna first. "Be very careful, bring plenty of firepower and go out to the Graham's hideaway. The assassins are Russian professional hit men that will not stop until they find her. I will be calling for more backup". He then called his contact in the regional FBI office, "You've heard about the shootings in Lake Worth Beach. I just got off a call from Interpol, and there may still be Russian assassins on the loose after Mrs. Graham. It's a long story, but I need FBI protection now at the following address. Don't take no for an answer. Later, we may need to talk about witness protection. This request Is going to come from the President tomorrow." Finally, Jack called Guthrie, and told him the news. "This puts a completely different slant on the investigation", moaned Guthrie. "Didn't we have enough problems all ready". "I am sorry to ruin your night, but we need to get everything we can on a Russian national named Victor Sidorov in Palm Beach or the Miami area. I already called my contact at the FBI, and they will help. Mrs. Graham is the target because of her family ties to a Ukrainian General. I will see you in the morning, and we'll try to sort it out". "Thanks for nothing", said Guthrie, and cut the phone connection.

The next morning, Jack went to the Sheriff substation on Lucerne Street, while Anna went back to the Graham hideaway to provide protection until backup could arrive. She brought her 9mm pistol, a shotgun and a bullet proof vest. She told Mr. and Mrs. Graham to stay away from windows and told them about the Russian sniper on the loose.

Jack walked into the substation, saw the receptionist and was ushered up the elevator to Detective Guthrie's office. He told him what he had learned the previous night from the Interpol phone call. "We need to find out if this Sidorov has been in Palm Beach, and if he is still here. We also need to put out an APB on Sergei Uryeva. I have asked the FBI to issue a stop order on Uryeva's passport, but that won't mean much if they take a private plane".

Guthrie did a quick search of the Property Appraiser's records for Victor Sidorov. He just completed a $110 million mansion in Palm Beach. It covers five acres from the ocean to the intracoastal. He did a quick Google maps search that brought up both overhead and street views of the mansion. It was a 30,000 square foot, four story modern glass and concrete structure, with large windows on the upper floors looking over the ocean, and large windows on all floors in the rear looking over the intracoastal. It had taken two years to build and looked like a modern art museum. A check of building records showed that there were 20 bedrooms, 25 baths, a great room, banquet hall, game rooms, swimming pool and offices. A 250-foot mega-yacht was docked behind the mansion.

Jack said, "it will take an army to get into that place. They probably have a private army of Spetsnaz soldiers besides the assassin". Detective Guthrie added, "he will have another army of lawyers ready to keep us out unless we have ironclad evidence. No one will challenge them based on the information we have now. The FBI will not want to start an international incident. Besides, the Sheriff closed the case, and would be embarrassed if we reopened it. I don't need that kind of attention. If we had evidence that Sergei killed Cameron, and evidence that Sergei was still working for Sidorov, we might have a chance." Jack muttered, "you don't want much". Guthrie replied, "I will check ballistics on the 9mm bullet that killed Dmitri, and the 308 rifle bullet that killed Cameron to see if there is a match to any previous crimes. That is as much as I can do".

Jack said, "Anna and I will do some surveillance of the mansion to see if Sidorov or Sergei are still there. Let me know if you hear anything else". He walked out of the substation and called Anna. "We need to use your boat tonight for some surveillance. Are the FBI agents protecting the Grahams?" "Yes, I can get away this afternoon. I will meet you at the marina about 6:00 pm. Bring supper, wine and snacks".

CHAPTER 42:
SURVEILLANCE

Jack drove his BMW down Federal Highway to the marina and parked in their parking lot. He pulled out a collapsible cart and filled it with groceries and drinks for the evening. He also pulled out an equipment bag filled with equipment they might need for the surveillance. He walked down to the finger docks pulling the cart and carrying the bag. As he approached the Catalina sailboat, he saw Anna sitting in the cockpit. "Permission to come aboard?" he said. Anna replied, "Sure. It looks like we are in for a long night".

Anna quickly cast off the lines from the dock, with Jack's help, and they got underway. They motored north at a leisurely 5 knots from the marina. They had to wait for the bridge to go up at the Lantana Bridge and again at the Lake Worth bridge. There was very little boat traffic as they motored north in the intracoastal. They went by the Lake Worth Golf Course, the Graham mansion with the burned-out hulk of the yacht, the C-51 canal between Lake Worth and West Palm Beach and many beautiful mansions on the water. As the sun was setting, they arrived off the Sidorov mansion on Palm Beach Island. It was clearly visible from the intracoastal waterway. Anna turned eastward out of the channel, and worked her way closer to the mansion, as if she were getting out of the channel to anchor for the night. They dropped anchor in about 8 feet of water and let out enough anchor line to assure the anchor would not pull out during the night. Then they made dinner and ate it at the table in the cockpit. They even had a bottle of wine that Jack had brought, and candles. It was a beautiful sunset as they finished dinner, and their hands found each other across the table.

Jack said, "it is wonderful just being out here with you. I was really scared when I heard you had been shot in the hospital. You mean a lot to me." Anna smiled and said, I thought this dinner was a little over the top for a stake-out." Jack laughed and said, "my timing stinks, but I needed to tell you how I feel about you. I love you Anna and don't want to lose you." They kissed for a long lingering moment that was not made up in case they were being watched. Anna said breathlessly, "You really know how to pick a romantic moment. I wondered if you would ever notice me as a woman instead of an investigator. That kiss tells me you definitely noticed. I love you too, you big lug. But we need to hold that thought until the work is done." She kissed Jack playfully, and then started gathering up their dishes.

When they had finished, they took the dishes down the ships ladder to the galley, washed them and made it look like they were settling in for an early night. Instead, they changed into black outfits, checked their surveillance equipment, and waited until it was completely dark. Then they came back out into the cockpit bringing the surveillance equipment.

Jack had a digital camera with a telescopic lens and night vision, a dish listening device and an infra-red camera to detect people inside the mansion. He also had a quadcopter drone with a camera that could take close-ups from above. It had limited battery life, so they would only launch it if they saw something useful. Jack watched the mansion and grounds for the first half hour. He saw two teams of guards with rifles, circling the house at set times. He also saw a dog with one of the teams. He muttered, "getting into that mansion will take a seal team". Once they had seen the initial security layout, Jack said, "we can take 2 hour shifts until 2:00 am. If we haven't seen anything by then, we probably won't. Remember that they have a very good sniper,so keep noise or light to a minimum". Anna shuddered, but said, "I will take the first shift. Get some rest and then relieve me". Jack went back into the cabin, and slept in the side berth in the main cabin, so that he would not be far away if he was needed. The night was dark, and Anna could see thousands of stars as she sat in the darkness. She thought about how different she felt about Jack tonight as she focused on the mansion with the camera. She had an earpiece to monitor the dish listening device and watched the infrared camera image of the mansion interior. Everything was also recorded so that they could use it as evidence if they were lucky. There were a few lights on in the mansion, but no indication of movement, except for the circling guards. Anna's shift passed slowly without incident, and she was glad to hear Jack as he came up the ship's ladder to the cockpit. He was carrying a mug of coffee, and had enough snacks to go to the movies. "I hope you have better luck than I did", she said as she got up, stretched and went down the ship's ladder to the rear cabin, which was where she slept normally.

Jack watched the mansion as lights went out in the other Palm Beach mansions. He shifted his position and looked at the stars as a distraction from watching nothing happen. It was about 11:30 pm, and everything was quiet. Then he saw lights being switched on inside the second floor. He sat up and focused the camera on three shadows. He could see three infra-red images inside the house on the infra-red monitor. A sliding door was pulled back and three people came out onto one of the balconies. A man and woman were arm in arm as they looked at the water and the stars. A third man stayed in the background with a rifle. Jack took closeup pictures of all three, and then launched the quadcopter from the other side of the cockpit. The drone rose to 500 feet, so its sound would be undetectable. He maneuvered the drone within about 100 feet of the house, so that it could take pictures from above. The dish picked up mumbled conversation as the couple embraced. As they separated, he heard, "Oh Victor, why do we have to move again. I like it here". Victor replied, "you will like it in Monte Carlo also. My business here is done, and we will be flying to Monte-Carlo in two days. Let's enjoy the evening". He raised his glass and they both drank their champagne, then the two went back inside, followed by their bodyguard. Jack hit the control to bring the drone back to the boat and waited for it to come down. He and Anna continued the surveillance until 2 am, but nothing else was seen or heard. "We will check the recorded sound and video in the morning before weighing anchor. Let's get some sleep".

Jack let Anna go down into the cabin first, admiring her figure, even with the black clothing. As he came down the ladder, Anna turned and held out her hand. Her hair was down and he felt his heart jump as he held it. He reached for her and she was in his arms. They kissed deeply, and she said "Oh Jack, I have been waiting for this". He kissed her again, and his hands moved under the black clothes. They came up for air, and Anna gently pulled him back to the rear cabin. As they closed the door to the main cabin, clothes were flying off both bodies. They fell into bed, and soon the boat was rocking rhythmically.

The next morning, Jack and Anna slept late, and came into the main cabin hand in hand. They made coffee and then breakfast, which they shared in the cockpit. Their eyes and smiles showed something had changed between them. Jack said, "That bed was very nice, but I did bump my head a few times. It might be more comfortable if you stayed with me in the Green Bungalow". Anna laughed quietly and replied, "I think I would like that, with one or two caveats". Jack said, "what do you mean"? " I have seen the Green Bungalow. It is a perfectly good bachelor pad, but if I am going to live there, it needs a major cleaning, and the number of liquor bottles needs to be reduced". Jack scratched his head, and said, "I think I could make those modifications if we had a few nights like last night." He pulled Anna to him and kissed her.

After breakfast, they turned to business and checked the computer. They watched the video and listened to the sound recording from the previous night. Although the images were dark, there was enough light to see the faces of all three people on the balcony. The voice recording clearly picked up the name Victor and the plans for leaving. They then made a show of weighing anchor and motoring on up to West Palm Beach under the Southern Blvd and Okeechobee Blvd bridges. They pulled into the West Palm Beach pier for the day, and left the boat. Anna would come back that afternoon and sail the boat back to the marina. Jack had called Detective Guthrie that morning and sent copies of the video and sound recording to him for further analysis. They took an Uber to the Sheriff Substation to see Guthrie, and decide on the next step.

CHAPTER 43:
FINAL PLANS

When Jack and Anna walked into the substation conference room, Detective Guthrie looked up and saw the light shining in their eyes. He thought, they finally got together, but didn't say anything. He said, "we have been analyzing the video and sound recordings from last night. It is hard to make an identification from the videos, but the name Victor is clear, and the intent to leave the country." Jack said, "That mansion is defended like Fort Knox. It has both electronic and personnel security". Guthrie replied," after the debacle with Cameron at the Boca airport, I will not be able to get a SWAT team to help on this one. We have a warrant out for Sergei for the murder of Dmitri and arson on the car. That would give us a reason to stop him, but we have nothing on Sidorov". Jack asked, "have you been able to check calls between the two?" "They are encrypted, and we haven't been able to break into them". Jack said, "let me make a call". He called his FBI contact and asked, "can you get some help from NSA to break some encrypted calls between Sergei Yureava and Victor Sidorov? They are suspected of several murder plots in Palm Beach County, and they are a flight risk". "I know someone in NSA. Let me see what I can do." Detective Guthrie said, "we checked with the State Department and Sidorov does not have a diplomatic passport. If he did, we couldn't touch him. Even without diplomatic immunity, we need an iron clad case to prevent an international incident. Neither you nor I could stand that kind of heat". They broke for lunch at Murray's, and decided to meet again at 5:00 pm. Anna left to take the Catalina back to the marina. Jack checked with the Graham security detail, and found that everything was quiet.

Jack received a phone call from his FBI contact about 4:00 pm. "I pushed NSA hard, and you owe me a bottle of Maker's Mark the next time you are in DC". Jack agreed, and said "what did you find out"? "There has been a lot of phone traffic between Victor and Dmitri earlier, and then between Victor and Sergei. The calls were within 24 hours before each of the murders, including the last one of Cameron. There were also calls from the assassins back to Victor within a few hours of the murders, reporting on them. Clearly, Victor Sidorov is the mastermind behind all of these murders. There were also several calls from a high-ranking Russian FSB agent to Sidorov during the last two months. Sidorov was taking orders from the Russians. That amounts to espionage. Now the FBI has a reason to move in. I will call you back in two hours with instructions".

Jack went back to the Sheriff substation at 5:00 pm and reported the FBI conversation to Detective Guthrie. Guthrie did not want to bring in the top brass again until they knew the FBI plans. "I have seen these things fall apart when FBI top brass are involved", he said. They talked about how they could take down Sidorov and Sergei with the least chance for an international incident. "We already disrupted the Boca airport when we went after Cameron," said Guthrie. "The FAA will not stand for a shootout at Palm Beach International. It has too many major airlines and high-powered executives coming and going". Jack said, "I have seen the external security at the Sidorov mansion, and I am sure he did not scrimp on electronic security either. The mansion cannot be breached without a full-fledged Army Rangers or Navy Seals team. The SWAT team would be out gunned. When Sidorov goes to the airport he will have a major security escort. We don't want a firefight in the middle of Palm Beach". Both Jack and Guthrie got up and had another cup of coffee.

When Jack sat down at the conference table again, he said, "what about the bridge"? Guthrie said, "there are several bridges from Palm Beach to West Palm Beach. We can't cover all of them". Jack replied, "the obvious choice to go to the airport is the Southern Blvd bridge. It is under construction now, and has a temporary metal bridge over the intracoastal. When Sidorov's motorcade turns onto the Southern Blvd approach to the bridge, they are committed. We can have a watch on the mansion and alert our forces at the bridge to be ready. Once they are on Southern, we pull trucks to block the road after them. We can also raise the bridge to prevent them breaking through. We can have boats in the water to prevent them escaping on the water. We may have some civilians on the road, depending on the time, and we will have to evacuate them from the area before approaching the motorcade, but it is the best chance to limit risk and casualties when we take Sidorov and Yureava down. We will have to be ready for a major firefight, with SWAT teams on both ends of the bridge, and a sniper in the bridge control house".

Detective Guthrie thought that over and said, "what about a helicopter transfer to the airport? I know they would not flinch at the cost of a helicopter". Jack grimaced, and then said, "we can take advantage of Mr. Trump staying at Mar-a-lago, and have the FAA ground all helicopter flights for the next two days. All of Palm Beach is used to restrictions caused by Mr. Trump, even though he is no longer the president". Guthrie thought it over and nodded, "it could work that way, but we would need a lot of manpower. Let's see what the FBI says". They walked from the substation down to Murray's on Lake Avenue, since it was officially past Guthrie's work hours. Over a beer they talked more about the possible options and repercussions of each strategy.

At 7:00 pm, Jack's phone rang. His FBI contact told him the warrant for Sidorov had been issued for espionage and conspiracy to commit murder. "This was approved by the FBI director, and it will go to the White House tomorrow morning. You had better be right about this or both of our careers and lives will be in jeopardy. The FBI regional director for Southeast Florida is taking charge of this directly, and you will both report to him tomorrow morning by 10:00 am in West Palm Beach. In the meantime, we will maintain surveillance on the mansion and anyone leaving it". Jack thought as he said goodbye to Guthrie, "Anna and I may need to relocate to Key West in her Catalina sooner than I thought".

The next morning, Jack and Anna couldn't stop smiling at each other, as they drove the BMW to the FBI headquarters at 505 S Flagler Blvd in West Palm Beach. The building was a fifteen story white stone tower, with windows looking out over the downtown and the intracoastal waterway. The tower was just north of two higher white towers that had previously been named "Trump Towers" before his presidential election run. The name had been removed due to democratic sentiment.

After parking in a parking garage, Jack and Anna entered the building, showed their credentials and were ushered up to the sixth floor, and into a very large conference room that was rapidly filling up. They took advantage of the coffee and found a place around the conference table.

A distinguished looking man in his fifties, followed by four serious looking suits, walked in and took their places at reserved seats in the center of the conference table. Detective Guthrie, the Sheriff and the West Palm Beach police chief trailed them in and took their assigned seats. At the appointed time, The FBI Regional Director rose and introduced himself. "Gentlemen and ladies, I am FBI Director West of the Southeast Region. I am in command of this operation as of now. The FBI has learned that a Russian Oligarch, Victor Sidorov, has been living in Palm Beach for several months at a home on Palm Beach. Mr. Sidorov has recently been implicated in Russian espionage and murder investigations, along with at least two of his bodyguards. This situation has been classified at the highest levels, and shall not be shared with anyone outside this room, do I make myself clear"? He looked over the conference table for emphasis. "As of this morning, the President has been briefed and has given the go ahead to arrest Mr. Sidorov in accordance with the warrants issued by a Federal Judge. The arrest must be made with a minimum of risk and collateral damage to surrounding facilities. We have reviewed several options, and are currently developing plans for this action. If anyone has reservations or alternatives, raise them now before we finalize the plans today. We do not know when Mr. Sidorov will attempt to leave the country, but we must be ready by midnight tonight at the latest. I will now call on Detective Captain Guthrie of the Sheriff Department to provide a more detailed description of the plan, and assignments for the takedown. "

Detective Guthrie rose from his seat, looking pale. He outlined the three options that he and Jack had considered, and the reasons why the Southern Avenue bridge was the best option. The rest of the day was consumed with questions, alternatives and reservations to the plan, but in the end, it was the one selected. FBI SWAT teams would take the lead in the takedown of the Sidorov motorcade. Jack, Anna and two FBI agents would act as lookouts in a vehicle parked close to the Sidorov mansion. SWAT teams would be located at the Southern bridge, and in armored vehicles just north of the Southern bridge on A1A. The armored vehicles would follow the Sidorov motorcade onto the causeway. Detective Guthrie and several deputies would ride in an SUV behind the SWAT team. A flat bed tractor trailer filled with concrete barriers would block the two lanes behind the Sidorov motorcade, SWAT team and Sheriff vehicles. The FBI would take over the operation of the bridge from the normal bridge tender. Snipers would be located in the towers on both sides of the bridge. In addition, Sheriff and Coast Guard boats would be hidden in marinas on both sides of the bridge and across from the Sidorov mansion until the motorcade was stopped on the bridge. Then they would cover potential escape routes if boats left the mansion or if people jumped from the causeway. The WPB Police chief took responsibility for evacuating vehicles stopped on the bridge causeway. Hopefully, this would be done before the motorcade itself was approached. A Sheriff helicopter would provide an overview of the operation for the Sheriff and Director West. It was hoped that the massive show of force at the bridge would prevent a firefight, but everyone had to be ready if the spetsnaz bodyguards opened fire. As a precaution, all other bridges over the intracoastal waterway from West Palm Beach to Boynton Beach would be opened at the same time as the Sidorov motorcade left the mansion.

Director West closed the meeting at 2:00 pm and said, "everyone be ready and in place by 11:00 pm tonight. We must be ready, if Sidorov makes a move."

At the Sidorov mansion, final plans were also being made. Sidorov, his wife and his bodyguard Sergei knew that the FBI was closing in. The Russians had moles in the FBI headquarters in Washington. Sidorov had received an encrypted phone call that morning warning him to get out of Palm Beach. His request for a helicopter had been denied due to potential conflicts with ex-President Trump. That meant he would need to travel by motorcade. His armored limousine would be led by two black Suburban SUVs filled with Spetnaz guards. There would also be two SUVs behind the limo to slow down any FBI chases. His plane was ready for an immediate departure once they entered the airport. He would have his yacht leave five minutes before the motorcade to draw off any pursuit. He asked Sergei, "is there anything else we can do to escape?" Sergei said, "let me think about that."

CHAPTER 44:
TAKEDOWN

That night at 11:00 pm, everyone was in place and trying to be inconspicuous, so that word would not get back to the Russians. FBI Director West, the Sheriff and the West Palm Beach Police Chief were in a FBI Command Post on the tenth floor of the FBI Building on Flagler Avenue in West Palm Beach. They had a clear view of the bridge scene and communications with all of the FBI and Sheriff units. Everyone was keyed up, but they knew this would likely be a long wait. The night passed slowly, and lookouts near the Sidorov mansion and his plane at Palm Beach International airport had nothing to report.

About 10:00 am, the lookouts at the airport reported that two pilots and an attendant walked out to the Sidorov Boeing 737, to begin their pre-flight preparations. The plane was always fueled and provisioned as soon as it landed, so that it would be ready for the next flight. About 11:00 am, Jack and the lookouts at the mansion reported that the gates opened and a large motorcade was leaving. It Included two black Suburbans in the lead filled with guards, the limousine carrying Sidorov and his mistress, and two black Suburbans bringing up the rear. The motorcade turned north toward the Southern Blvd bridge. Everyone checked their equipment, and got ready as the motorcade approached. The gates on the east bound traffic were closed to stop traffic coming onto the causeway from the west. When the Sidorov motorcade pulled around the traffic circle at A1A and Southern Blvd onto the bridge causeway, a lookout alerted the SWAT team to start moving. The armored vehicles pulled onto the causeway side by side to block both lanes of traffic. Detective Guthrie's SUV was next followed by the flat bed truck that blocked both lanes of the causeway near the Southern traffic circle. Even a fast moving SUV would not move that truck. The bridge tender closed all of the gates and opened the bridge. As the bridge started to move up, everyone in the motorcade realized they were trapped. The West Palm Beach officers approached the three cars stopped in front of the motorcade in full riot gear with shields. They removed the car occupants and took them to a construction container where they would be safe. So far, no one had approached the motorcade or left it. Now the FBI SWAT teams from before and after the motorcade approached it. They called for all of the occupants to leave their vehicles with their hands up and lay on the ground with their hands behind their heads. This was the critical moment, and they expected a barrage of bullets at any time.

196

Instead, the doors of the vehicles slowly opened and people started to comply with the orders. A man in an expensive coat and a young woman left the limousine and stood beside it with their hands up. The SWAT team and Detective Guthrie moved toward them to take them into custody. As they got close to the limousine, Guthrie got a good look at the man and woman. "That is not Sidorov," he yelled. "This is a set-up." He quickly looked in the limousine and confirmed it was empty. "Where is Sidorov?" he asked the man. "I am Mr. Sidorov's attorney and I strenuously object to this violation of his and my rights. The Kremlin will hear about this outrage. We have done nothing wrong." Guthrie radioed back to the command helicopter that Sidorov was not there. "Where could he have gone?" said Director West. "Have you heard anything further form the lookout at the mansion?" "No, but I will contact them," said Guthrie. He had a sinking feeling in his stomach that this would be his last day as a detective. He called Jack Price but couldn't get an answer.

CHAPTER 45:

SHOOTOUT

Jack, Anna and the two deputies had been assigned as lookouts at the Sidorov mansion. Jack was driving a black FBI SUV and they were parked in a driveway just south of the mansion. Jack was not thrilled to be sidelined away from the action at the takedown, but he accepted his assignment. When the motorcade left the mansion and went north on the two lane road called A2A, he had reported it to Guthrie and had listened on the radio to the action on Southern Blvd. Anna and the two deputies wanted to tail the motorcade and be part of the takedown, but Jack didn't want to abandon his assigned post.

Five minutes after the motorcade left, Jack saw a Bentley sedan followed by a white van leave from the Sidorov mansion and go south instead of north. The white van had a ladder rack and two ladders on its top. Jack recognized the van from the shooting at the Boca Raton airport. He said, "Something is not right here. No one drives a Bentley unless they are a billionaire, and that van is the same one I saw when Cameron was shot at the Boca Raton airport.

We are going to follow them." He pulled out onto A1A and stayed about two blocks behind the white van. He tried to call Guthrie to warn him that the motorcade might be a distraction, but Guthrie did not answer the phone. He asked Anna to keep calling Guthrie as he drove. They followed the van south on A1A until they reached the Lake Worth bridge. He did not want to be recognized and start a police chase on A1A, which is normally a quiet residential street providing access to the Palm Beach mansions with a speed limit of 30 mph and many bicycles enjoying the beautiful views. He hoped that all of the bridges south of Southern Blvd had heeded the orders to open the bridges and block the road.

The first bridge he came to was Lake Worth bridge. Both the east and west bound lanes were blocked by the opened bridge. He stopped near the bridge, pulled out a set of binoculars and looked for the van. The traffic was very heavy, and it was clear everyone would have to wait a long time even if the bridge closed, so the Bentley and the van kept driving south. Jack confirmed that the van was not on the approach to the bridge, so he gunned the SUV and roared through the stop light down A1A. He called ahead to ask the Boynton police to block A1A south of the Boynton Beach bridge to keep the Bentley and van from escaping to the south.

The next bridge was a beautiful new bridge on Lantana Blvd. The bridge was a two-lane bridge with the bridge tender's tower on the west side of the bridge. There was a long two-lane approach road on the east side. The bridge approach had concrete barriers between lanes to prevent people pulling into the oncoming lane when the bridge was up. The bridge was up, blocking traffic and causing a traffic jam. Cars were angrily honking their horns at the bridge tender because the bridge had been up for longer than usual. Jack again pulled out his binoculars and saw a white van on the approach to the bridge heading west. He turned onto Lantana, going the wrong way on the eastbound lanes of the road and stopped the SUV just past a shopping center. He called out to the others, "Everybody out and get geared up for a firefight." They opened the back double doors, and each put on a protective vest with ceramic plates over the chest to stop bullets. They added ballistic helmets with built in radios for communication. They picked out long guns from a stack of AR-15s, machine pistols and sniper rifles. Thay also checked their service pistols and spare clips. When they were ready, they piled back in the SUV and Jack told Anna to call Guthrie and let him know that they were going after the Bentley and Sidorov. Anna finally got through and updated Guthrie. She asked for immediate backup and for the helicopter to provide overhead information. Guthrie said to stay where they were until the SWAT teams arrived, but Jack was afraid the bridge tender would cave to the angry horns and let the bridge down soon. Jack drove the SUV the wrong

200

way up the bridge approach, over a small bridge and started up the empty eastbound lanes of the bridge approach to close in on the van. As he approached, he told everyone to be ready for a firefight.

When he was about 300 feet behind the van, the van's driver saw him coming in his mirror. He opened the driver's side door and sprayed the SUV with a Russian automatic pistol. The bullets broke the windshield, and sprayed broken glass over Jack, Anna and the deputies. Jack stopped the SUV and told Anna to cover them with the sniper rifle from the top of the SUV. He and the two deputies jumped out, ducked down and started moving up along the concrete barriers between the two lanes toward the van. This was a treacherous situation since there were people caught in their vehicles behind the van that would be in the crossfire if Jack fired on the van. People were screaming and either ducking down inside their vehicles or running back down the bridge approach alongside the vehicles in the west bound lane. Jack and the deputies did not approach the van until most of the people had gotten away from the scene. Jack saw the Sheriff helicopter circle over the bridge and heard over the radio that the FBI SWAT teams were on their way. He radioed for Guthrie to make sure the bridge tender did not lower the bridge and said they would wait for backup unless forced to act.

Suddenly, two bodyguards opened the rear of the van, and fired with their automatic rifles. Jack and the two deputies returned fire while being careful not to hit the passenger cars. Jack caught one of the guards with two rounds in the chest and neck before he could empty his magazine. The deputies were firing from behind the concrete barrier. Jack saw the passenger door of the van open and a guard ran up the far side of the stopped vehicles toward the bridge. He opened the passenger door of one of the vehicles and pulled out a woman as a hostage, Jack called a halt to the firing because he could not endanger the hostage. The guard yelled for Jack to have the bridge tender lower the bridge or he would shoot a hostage every minute. Jack yelled back, "we can't contact the bridge tender that quickly. Give us five minutes." The guard yelled, "I will give you five dead hostages." Jack called Anna to see if she had a shot. "I can take out the guard at the back door on your call, but I don't have a shot at the guard with the hostage. Jack bent double and started to run toward the van. The concrete barrier kept him from being seen. When he had sneaked past the van and the Bentley, he peaked above the barrier to spot the guard with the hostage. The guard was looking back toward the deputies' location and had not seen Jack. He held the hostage close to him and faced back toward the van. Jack whispered over the radio, "I will free the hostage and then you take the guard in the back of the van." Anna hissed "Roger." Jack dropped his rifle and pulled his pistol from his shoulder holster. He counted to himself, "3, 2, 1." He raised up smoothly, like he was in the shooting range, and smoothly fired the pistol twice into the guard's head. The guard fell back, and the hostage screamed, but she was alright. He heard a rifle shot almost immediately and knew the guard at the rear of the van was down. He swung the pistol toward the Bentley three vehicles behind the hostage's vehicle and fired two shots through the driver's side windshield.

The passenger door to the Bentley opened and Sergei jumped out. Using the door as a shield. He fired an automatic 9mm pistol at Jack before Jack could duck behind the concrete barrier. Jack felt two bullets stitch a path up his chest and a third bullet hit his left arm, spinning him around. The impact of the three bullets knocked him back and he fell behind the concrete barrier. Sergei came around the front of the Bentley to finish him off. He recognized Jack and knew he had been responsible for stopping the getaway. This was now personal instead of being about his master. As Sergei approached, he moved past the line of cars and leaned over the concrete barrier to finish Jack. Jack looked up into his eyes and knew that this was the end. He was sorry that he was leaving Anna so soon. He closed his eyes and waited for the bullet. A rifle cracked. Jack opened his eyes and saw what was left of Sergei's head looking down at him where Sergei had fallen onto the concrete barrier. He couldn't believe he was still alive. Anna had seen Sergei move and had a clear shot as he went past the line of cars. Jack tried to get up but fell back to the ground.

The van driver leaned out of his door and fired a long burst back at Anna. Bullets flew around her and slammed into the top of the FBI SUV. She ducked to shield her face from the metal splinters but felt several pieces of shrapnel hit her arms. The deputies beside the concrete barrier returned fire at the van driver. One of the deputies hit the driver of the van and he went down on the pavement. Quickly, a white rag was waved out the rear passenger side door of the Bentley. After the shooting stopped, the two armored FBI SWAT team vehicles rolled up the empty east bound lanes of the bridge approach. The SWAT teams took control of the scene and carefully advanced on the Bentley and van, which were now riddled with bullets. They called for everyone to get out of the vehicles with their hands up and lay on the ground with their hands behind their heads. When they got close to the van, they could see all three of the bodyguards had been hit. When they got to the Bentley, they found Victor Sidorov was in the rear passenger seat of the car waving a white rag. His mistress was huddled on the floor of the rear seat, where she had taken refuge from the gunfire. They pulled Sidorov and his mistress from the Bentley, and pushed them to the ground, making sure he was no longer armed. They were cuffed and then guarded while they sat on the pavement next to the Bentley.

Detective Guthrie arrived with three additional deputies in another black SUV with flashing blue lights. Two ambulances from the Fire Department were right behind him. When Guthrie got out of the SUV, he could see the two deputies near the concrete barrier. One was down and the other was trying to give first aid. He then saw two bodies further up the road by the concrete barrier. He motioned for the two first ambulance crews to help them first. He told his deputies to check all of the cars on the bridge approach and determine if there were additional casualties. Then he saw a figure lying on top of the Black SUV behind him. He sent one of the deputies to check them. From the number of bullet holes visible he couldn't believe the ferocity of the firefight and the chaos it had caused. He could see where bullets had scarred the fresh paint on the new bridge, and he knew that he would be facing many questions about why he had allowed this carnage to occur near so many public vehicles. He could imagine the newspaper stories and the lawsuits that would come later. But they had caught both Sergei and Victor Sidorov.

He had Victor and his mistress helped across the concrete barriers and then placed inside an armored SWAT vehicle with two SWAT team members guarding them. They were then taken to the County jail. Guthrie called for the deputies to secure a crime scene 300 feet from the bridge on the east approach road. No vehicles would be allowed to leave, and all people would be interviewed before they could leave. He walked around the van and the Bentley and called for an immediate CSI team to photograph and process the scene before any of the bodies were removed. He also called for the County Emergency Response Command Center to be brought to the scene, since he knew the number of agencies that would soon descend onto the scene.

Anna, Jack and the injured deputy were bandaged and then rushed to JFK hospital in ambulances. The injured deputy had serious wounds to his shoulder and a concussion from a bullet hitting his helmet. Jack was bruised where the two bullets had hit the ceramic plates that saved his life. He also had a broken arm from the third shot. Anna had cuts in her arms from the shrapnel caused by flying bullets. She was treated and released. The bodies of the guards were taken to the morgue for autopsies, although everyone knew their cause of death.

Before long the Lantana bridge area was a mass of flashing lights, cameras, reporters and agencies investigating the shootout. FBI Director West arrived and took overall command from the Mobile Command Center. The sheriff, FBI and news station helicopters circled the bridge taking photographs and video. The reporters were on national news with the story, and the internet was on fire with differing opinions. It took three days to process the scene and remove the vehicles so the bridge could be returned to service. The investigation would take months before a final report was issued.

EPILOGUE
SIX MONTHS LATER

It was a beautiful sunny day with a nice breeze coming from the east. Jack and Anna were sailing north on Anna's 32-foot Catalina. The mainsail and jib were set, and Anna was steering the wheel with one foot, as she laid back in Jack's arms in the cockpit. They both had a wine glass, and a bottle was half full on the cockpit table. She said, "this is the way life is supposed to be". Jack had recovered from his injuries, and was sporting a few more scars on his arm and face. "It makes you look more like a pirate", Anna said as she smiled up at him. Anna had moved in with Jack in the Green bungalow shortly after he was released from the hospital. They were still adjusting to each other's routines, but were deliriously happy with each other. The Catalina was still in the marina, but it was confined to being used for day sailing now.

As they sailed north after going under the Lantana and Lake Worth bridges, they talked about the shootout with Sidorov and Sergei Yureva. "They almost outsmarted us", said Jack. "If they had used a regular car or different colored van, I probably would not have guessed that something was wrong until it was too late. If they had taken off in Sidorov's plane, we couldn't have touched them". Sergei and all of the bodyguards were killed in the shootout on the Lantana bridge. The other bodyguards that were with the motorcade will be convicted of various lesser crimes and imprisoned. The Russian mastermind, Victor Sidorov, was convicted of the murder of the developer, Cameron, conspiracy to commit murder and espionage related to the plot on Mrs. Graham and the threats against the Ukrainian general. Before he could be imprisoned, he was released to the Russians as part of a prisoner exchange for a Ukrainian diplomat and a female soccer player. Jack still hadn't gotten over that political decision, but he didn't have a say in the outcome. He wasn't sure if Sidorov was going back to a Russian dacha and his old life, or a bullet in the forest.

Mr. and Mrs. Graham were placed in the federal witness protection program, to protect them from future Russian assassins and Graham's mafia connections. Their mansion on the intracoastal was sold, and Mr. Graham sold his lucrative law office. Facing a new life outside the legal and modeling profession was enough of a penalty for the shady deals that Graham had made. As Jack and Anna sailed the Catalina north, they could see the repainted Graham mansion with a new yacht tied to its dock. Anna whispered, "life goes on, and they embraced."

Detective Guthrie was promoted from the Lake Worth substation to the chief of detectives for the county. Jack was happy for him, and sure that they would be asked to help with other cases in the future. The two deputies involved in the shootout, Jack and Anna had been recognized by the Sheriff for bravery in the face of extreme danger for their parts in the shootout. The story and pictures were picked up by local news stations, which did not hurt Jack and Anna's private investigation business.

Lake Worth Beach had a special election to elect two new commissioners to take the places of Commissioner Nichols and Peters. A Hispanic woman and a black man were elected to give better representation to those growing populations. Commissioner Nichols was given a 10-year sentence, and was currently serving it in South Bay Corrections Facility, a 2000 man maximum security prison in the glades area. It was hard to imagine two more different lifestyles than the one Nichols had been living and was living now just thirty miles west of Palm Beach.

Pastor Morris recovered from his wounds, sued the estate of James Cameron, the developer, and used the large financial settlement to improve his church and provide services to his parishioners. He also renamed the church, The Seminole Church of God, in honor of his ancestor, Aloyisus James. The land claim was framed and hanging prominently in the front of the church.

Jack and Anna had received a nice check from Mr. Graham for private investigation services, plus a bonus. The money was enough to do some long-needed upgrades in the green bungalow, so that Anna would be comfortable and happy there. If Anna was happy, Jack would be happy.

Lake Worth Beach had settled down somewhat after the murders, but it was still an eclectic community, with wide ranging lifestyles, economics and politics. As Jack watched the Palm Beach golf course drift by the boat, he smiled and thought, "That suits me just fine.

ABOUT THE AUTHOR

LARRY ALVA is the author of ASSASSINS, the first in a series of Lake Worth Mysteries. He is also author of THE GOOD NEWS IS LOVE, a non-fiction book about Love, Purpose and Hope while following Jesus.

Larry is an accomplished engineer, manager, inventor, woodworker, boater, and scuba diver. He lives in Florida with his wife and has two grown daughters and five grandchildren. They are his greatest legacy.

Larry spends his time writing, building furniture and clocks, making bowls and wood vases. He volunteers at his church, food distribution agencies and prison ministries.

Made in the USA
Columbia, SC
07 November 2023

25265230R00126